WRAITH'S REVENGE

RYAN KIRK

WATERSTONE
MEDIA

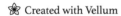 Created with Vellum

For Sangam

PROLOGUE

He sat, perfectly still, on a tree stump near the center of his garden. Years ago, he'd taken the time to saw, plane, and sand the stump until it was nearly as smooth as glass. Since then, it had become his favorite place to relax and meditate.

Songbirds chirped to one another as they nibbled on the seeds he'd left out for them this morning. He listened to the soft, quick flutter of their wings as they half-flew, half-hopped from seed to seed. They were grateful for the food as the winds grew colder.

Autumn had already passed through his garden. It had turned the leaves of his maples vibrant reds and oranges before they'd fallen. The flowers he tended so carefully through the spring and summer died under the relentless passage of the seasons, and he'd only completed the harvest of his vegetables a few days ago.

Today's stiff breeze cut through his thin tunic, but he did not shiver. He looked forward to the change of seasons. They served as a constant metaphor for life, and he welcomed the soft blanket of pure snow that settled in his garden. He would carefully shovel and sweep a narrow path from his back door to the stump, which he'd also keep clear all winter. Then he'd continue his routine of sitting on the stump and meditating.

In the winter, surrounded by the snow, he felt clean.

He could almost convince himself that his sins would someday be purified.

It was a lie, of course, but a pleasant one. The greatest gift he could offer was his own eternal soul, and that gift had already been given.

Far off in the distance, well beyond his sight, he heard a carriage bumping along the uneven set of tracks that served as a path to his house. The crack of a whip startled the birds and sent them flying to the higher branches of the maple.

He frowned. The carriage sounded heavier than his expected company. And there were more horses accompanying it than usual.

He uncrossed his legs and rose smoothly to his feet. He crossed his garden and went inside. His motions were calm and unhurried, but purposeful and efficient. Before long, a small fire warmed the water in his old kettle.

When the carriage stopped in front of his house, he stepped out to greet it.

Ten fully armored knights and an ornate carriage interrupted the endless vista of grass and shrubs. He recognized most of the knights, and gave them a brief bow, out of respect for their service.

The commander of the guards returned the bow with a nod of his own. He then gestured to one of his knights, who dropped off his horse and entered the house. They didn't bother to ask permission, but they didn't need it. He waited patiently as the knight conducted his search. The knight returned. "Empty, sir."

The commander gestured to the carriage attendants, who opened the door and rolled out a rug. Two weathered hands clasped the frame of the door for support. A ring weighed the hand down, bearing the burden of the world's most important office. A familiar face appeared, though it had been transformed by the passage of time.

His guest smiled. "Quinton, it's good to see you."

Quinton dropped to one knee and bowed his head. "Holy Father, the honor is all mine."

Father stepped down from the carriage, supported by both carriage attendants. Once he stood on the ground, though, he dismissed them. Quinton was glad to see Father still stood strong on his own, for if he fell, so did the church.

"Rise, Quinton. There is no need for such formality between us. It has been far too long, and I am eager to rest in your garden once more."

Quinton stood, and Father gestured for him to lead the way. Though it clearly pained the knight commander, the two proceeded without any escort.

The knight commander's distaste for the arrangement was perfectly reasonable, but he had nothing to fear. Quinton would die a hundred times before allowing Father to suffer so much as a scratch.

When they entered Quinton's house, he looked upon his barren dwellings in a new light. They weren't suitable to host someone like Father. He didn't have a single piece of art decorating the walls.

Father didn't seem perturbed by the lack of decoration. "Your dwellings reflect your continued focus, do they not?"

"They do, Father. I've found anything beyond the necessities to be nothing more than a distraction."

Father looked at the bare walls and noticed the kettle boiling. The corner of his mouth turned up in a smile. "I must confess that coming here feels like stepping into the past. Even you look the same."

Shame flushed Quinton's cheeks.

Father shook his head. "I'm sorry, Quinton. I did not mean to disparage you. The burden you bear on behalf of the church is perhaps even greater than my own. It is fitting you enjoy some small recompense for all that we ask of you."

The shame passed as quickly as it arrived. "The water is almost ready. Would you prefer to sit in the garden? I'll be out in a minute."

"I'd like that very much. Thank you."

Father stepped out the back door, and Quinton watched him through the window as he ambled toward the rear corner of the garden. Though Quinton never used the table, he kept it and the chairs as clean as everything else in his house. He saw the way Father's shoulders slumped as he relaxed into the chair.

Preparing the tea didn't take long. He took a small sip from his own cup to ensure it was worth being served, then carried a tray outside. He set it down on the table and poured Father a cup.

"Thank you," Father said.

"You're welcome."

"Even the table looks the same as it did when I was here last." Father gave him a knowing look. "You still prefer the stump, don't you?"

"I use the table when the cardinals check on me, but yes, I do. Sometimes, it feels like I can sense a connection with this world through it."

Father's gaze was sharp. "The cardinals report that your health remains unchanged."

Quinton understood his friend's concern. He held out

his hand, which was perfectly steady. Father relaxed at the sight, then leaned back in his chair. They both sipped their tea, and the birds returned to the seeds. Their presence delighted Father. "It is difficult to enjoy such serenity in the cities. Even the church grounds are too busy with visitors and services."

"I'm grateful for the house," Quinton said. He was curious about what, specifically, brought Father out here, but he sensed Father both desired and needed the quiet his garden provided.

When Father finished one cup of tea, Quinton poured him another. They watched the birds, and Quinton felt the familiar meditative state that was most of his existence set in.

Father sighed. "I could rest here for a long time."

"You are always welcome, of course."

Father finally broached the subject of his visit. "As I'm sure you've assumed, this is no mere social visit. I come with a task for you, I'm afraid."

Quinton set his teacup down. "You've come across someone so strong?"

"We have. He's killed knights, inquisitors, and even hosts. He's made enemies of both the Family and the church. We just learned that he's killed a cardinal outside of a growing town called Razin."

Quinton raised an eyebrow. His gaze wandered back to the house, where his sword rested in the corner. How long had it been since Father had given him a reason to draw it? Somewhere along the line, he'd lost track. "He must be strong to survive your retribution."

"He is. You'll read his story soon enough. He grew up in the sword schools, and he's a veteran with years of combat experience in the unnamed groups."

Quinton's fingers tingled, and it took him a few seconds to recognize the sensation.

Excitement.

"You wish for me to kill him?"

"Worse." Father paused, spinning the teacup in his hand. "I want you to destroy him." Father's voice was colder than the sudden breeze that blew through the barren branches of the maple tree. "He threatens all that we work for. I don't need to tell you how important it is."

Quinton already had some idea. In his decades of service to the church, they had only used him a handful of times, and usually his orders came from cardinals. He said nothing, though, not wanting to interrupt Father.

"We're close, Quinton. Closer than ever. Our scientists think they'll understand all the secrets of the demons within five years. They believe we can master them. If so, the church will direct the course of humanity for the next hundred years. Maybe for the next thousand. We just need to survive the next ten."

Father's voice was nearly a growl. "But this man has a remarkable tendency to interrupt some of our most precious experiments. Wherever he wanders, he sniffs us out."

"He's deliberately targeting us?" Quinton couldn't keep the surprise from his voice.

"We believe so, yes."

"How much do you know about him?"

Father gave a grim laugh. "A lot, and still not enough. We have all his military records, his sword school records, and dozens of reports from marshals from east to west. Once, he even fell into the hands of our inquisitors. He's left a trail of broken lives across the country. I brought all the papers in the carriage for you."

"I look forward to hunting him."

Father stood. "Good. A final caution, though. He's been up against some of our best. The Family's, too. He's the only one still walking on this side of the gates. I'll grant you access to every resource the church has, but please, be careful. He's not to be underestimated."

"He's never faced anyone like me before."

Father smiled. "That is true. It is that knowledge that allows me to sleep at night." Father gave him the slightest of nods, a true honor. "Thank you for your hospitality. Someday, I hope to return and tell you we have achieved all we set out to accomplish, and you can finally lay your burdens down."

Quinton imagined the day Father would allow him to commit suicide. He felt a thrill of pleasure at the thought. "I look forward to that day."

"As do I. Be careful, old friend. The church has never faced a more dangerous enemy."

1

Tomas belched and immediately regretted it. The food and ale in this wreck of a saloon hadn't tasted good on the way down, and the flavor didn't improve with the addition of stomach acid. He tried to raise his hand and gave up once it climbed about six inches off the bar.

He settled for shouting. Not that there was anyone to talk over. There was one other man at the bar, sitting as far away from Tomas as possible. A couple sat at a table in the corner. The woman kept glaring at Tomas' interruptions. Tomas couldn't care less. "I want 'nother one!"

The barkeep shook his head. "You've had plenty. I should have cut you off three drinks ago."

"But how else can I make the food taste good?"

The barkeep nodded toward the door. "If you can't see yourself out, my boys can help."

"Ahh, it's a fight you want, innit?" Tomas pounded his fist on the bar, but missed and hit his own leg. He didn't feel it, though, so he couldn't have hit himself too hard. He hoped.

"Boys!" the barkeep called.

Tomas held up his hands in mock surrender. The motion almost tipped him off the back of his stool. "Fine. If you don't want my gold, I'll just take it someplace else!"

"There is nowhere else, you ass."

Tomas ignored the comment. Someone had to teach these frontier folks about dignity. He stood up, and the world twisted around him. When he blinked, he was on the ground, staring at a grimy floor.

Had someone hit him? He pushed himself up, but as near as he could tell, no one stood nearby. He blinked, trying to clear the cobwebs from his head.

The "boys," as the barkeep called them, were two burly gentlemen who hadn't been boys for at least a decade. They stood at the door, keeping a wary eye on him. He might as well have been invisible to all the other patrons.

Fine, then.

He realized, a few steps from the door, that he hadn't paid for his drinks yet. He jammed his right hand into his pocket and pulled out enough coin to cover the drinks and a few more besides. Though he didn't know the first thing about hospitality, the barkeep still needed the money more than Tomas did. He put the coin on the nearest table and stumbled to the door.

One of the "boys" growled at him as he passed. "Best you not come back here, ever."

Tomas, who only came up to the boy's chest, poked him. "Don't think for a minute you can tell me what to do."

He sensed the other giant behind him shift his weight, and Tomas spun to meet the attack. But his body wasn't obeying his commands, and he soon felt a giant boot lodging itself firmly in his bottom. He flew off the saloon's front steps and into the street.

Fortunately, he didn't feel the impact. He lay for a moment, enjoying the feeling of the cool gravel against his face. Then he pushed himself up for the second time in as many minutes and glared at the boys, who seemed entirely unintimidated.

He brushed himself off, but even that motion threatened his precarious balance. Instead, he settled for taking a deep breath. Tolkin was high in the sky, and it was time for him to find a place to rest. His original plan had been to sleep in the rented rooms above the saloon, but he had the sneaking suspicion the rooms wouldn't be available to him anymore.

He looked up and down the street and tried to remember where he was. The town was so small it didn't even have a name. The whole place wasn't more than two dozen houses and businesses, though he'd seen enough unfinished construction to know it was booming. Just like every other frontier town.

There was nowhere else to stay. A quick glance confirmed that fact.

Oh well. He'd spent hundreds of nights out under the stars, and though the air was turning cold, tonight promised to be a beautiful night. He shrugged his shoulders, chose a direction at random, and started walking.

When he reached the edge of town, he saw a rider on a horse tearing toward the town at a full gallop. Tomas frowned. Not only was the rider tempting all the challenges of night riding, the sagani were unusually active in this area, too. The hours after dusk were some of their most active.

The rider pulled on his reins as he neared Tomas. He looked like he was about to offer greetings, but then his eyes went wide.

The man didn't seem like much. His horse was old, and his clothes looked like they should have been cut into scraps about two years ago. But he was digging through his pockets as though there were treasure inside. Instead of gold, though, he pulled out a sheet of paper. He held it up to Tolkin's moonlight, then looked down at Tomas.

Tomas swore.

"You're him!" The rider dismounted, threw the paper to the ground, and drew his sword. The blade was dull and dirty, the edge chipped in several places. Tomas would have dismissed the man if not for the dried blood running along the weapon.

"You're Tomas, right?" the man asked, suddenly less certain of himself. "Wanted dead or alive by pretty much everyone?"

"What if I told you I wasn't?" Tomas asked.

The man practically hopped from foot to foot with excitement. "I knew it! I'd heard you were heading this direction. With the money I'll earn from bringing you in, I'll finally be able to start a farm."

Tomas frowned. He wished the man would speak slower and quieter. His head was hurting.

"Now, are you going to come peacefully, or do we have to do this the hard way?"

The hard way? Tomas winced. He studied the man for a moment.

The rider was off balance, his weight shifting from foot to foot. His hands were sweaty, and he kept repositioning his grip on the hilt of his sword. The tip drew chaotic patterns in the air between them.

"Have you ever held a sword before?" Tomas asked.

The man hesitated, which told Tomas all he needed to know.

"Look," said Tomas, stepping forward. "You know that with that amount of money on my head, I'm very dangerous. So why don't you run the other way before you get hurt?"

The man gripped his sword so tight his knuckles turned white. "You're a criminal and deserve to be brought to justice." He paused. "And I need the money."

Tomas scratched at the back of his neck. "I've had a terrible couple of weeks," he said. "If it's money you need, how about I just give you all I have and we call it good?"

"How much do you have?"

Tomas rooted around in his pockets and pulled out all the coins remaining to him. He grimaced when he saw how little it was. It was hard to bribe others when he could barely afford a room.

The man glared and raised his sword.

Tomas took a step back and almost fell. He blinked fast and opened his eyes wide, trying, and failing, to focus on the man's posture and weapon.

"So, you going to come peacefully or not?" the man asked.

"Uh... not?"

The man shouted as he stepped forward and brought the sword above his head. Suddenly, he was right in front of Tomas, and Tomas sidestepped just in time to see the sword cut through the space he'd occupied just a moment ago.

Then he tripped over what felt like a log. The man's sword passed overhead as Tomas tumbled onto his rear. He saw no log anywhere near his feet and spent a good two seconds being confused how he'd fallen. Then the man shouted again, stabbing his sword down.

Tomas rolled, his stomach grumbling at the movement. The sword jammed into the gravel of the road, giving Tomas time to push himself to hands and knees.

His stomach chose that moment to rebel. He vomited all

over his hands and the road. The acidic bile burned his throat and the smell of it made his eyes water.

He found his feet just in time to watch his would-be assassin pull the sword from the road. The man charged him again, and Tomas wondered what the man's tired horse thought of this exchange. The thought made him giggle.

Then he swore as the rider barely missed with his next cut.

He couldn't track the man's motions.

"Elzeth, if you don't want to die here, I could use your help."

The angry sagani maintained his stubborn silence. Tomas didn't even feel him stir.

The man chopped wildly at Tomas, who stumbled and tripped backward. The chipped sword drew blood along Tomas' left arm.

"Elzeth!"

Nothing.

Tomas fell again. Who had littered this road with small logs? He landed in a sitting position, and the man raised his sword high, a triumphant grin on his face.

Drunk as he was, Tomas couldn't avoid even this fool's cut. All he could do was watch as the sword came down at his head.

2

———

At the last possible moment, a wave of strength filled Tomas' limbs. The hopeful bounty hunter slowed, as though he moved through water instead of air.

Tomas reached out with his left hand, catching the man's left wrist with ease. His newly strengthened arm had no problem halting the strike. He pulled the man closer, and as the bounty hunter fell, drove his open palm into the man's chin.

The bounty hunter collapsed in a heap beside Tomas.

The danger past, strength fled from his body, and he felt sicker than before. All he wanted was to lie down next to the bounty hunter and sleep for the rest of the night. Maybe through the next day, too.

But he couldn't. For one, his new friend wouldn't be unconscious that long, and Tomas suspected he wouldn't be any more reasonable when he woke. For another, the poster meant his likeness was already being spread around this area. The church was sparing no expense to catch him.

He carefully got to his feet, his stomach rumbling. He picked his way over to where the old horse patiently waited for its master. Tomas introduced himself to the creature. It snorted and walked a few paces away, turning its tail to Tomas.

He bent over and picked up the paper the man had dropped. Sure enough, he stared at a decent print of his face. It listed all his crimes, and he whistled softly at its length. Then he scratched his head. He was sure the list hadn't been this long before. The reward had gone up, too. If it went much higher, he'd have to consider turning himself in, just for the money.

Sparing no expense, indeed.

He squeezed his eyes shut, trying to quiet the pounding in his head. The marshals, church, and Family all wanted him dead. Given how close he'd come to visiting the gates tonight, it wouldn't be long before everyone could declare victory and call it a day.

Tomas showed his wanted poster to the horse's rear. "What do you think?"

The horse wisely kept its opinions to itself.

"Eh, you're about as talkative as Elzeth these days."

Tomas crumpled the paper and tucked it in the horse's saddlebags. He considered stealing the horse as recompense for his troubles, but his bounty hunter already seemed down on his luck. Not to mention, Tomas thought as he examined the horse again, it didn't look like the mount would carry him very far.

He made it five steps from the horse before his stomach gave up the fight. Vomit exploded from him as though from a bursting dam, and before long, his hands were on his knees, his whole body heaving and shaking.

Tomas let it come, remaining bent over until the last drop dribbled from his lips. Then he spit, straightened, and wiped his mouth with his sleeve.

Elzeth's deep dissatisfaction was sourer than the taste in his mouth.

Looking down at the pool of tonight's meal, he supposed he couldn't blame Elzeth much.

But he didn't care, either. There were some things about human life the sagani would never understand.

Thankfully, he was feeling a little better. Embracing the powers of a host always cleared some of the alcohol from his blood, and the cool night air would do the rest. He had a long night ahead of him, so he started the journey.

He followed the road for a while, mostly to put distance between him and the last town.

When the bounty hunter woke up, Tomas expected him to rush into town. But he didn't expect the man to ride out again tonight.

The rising of the sun would bring the danger. Perhaps the man would come alone, or perhaps he'd raise a posse to help him. Either way, Tomas wanted to be out of sight of the road by the time the sun came up.

After a few hours, he turned off the road, choosing to go right at random.

In his stupor, he lost track of time, but the sky was turning colors when he came across the small stream. He looked down at his hands, sniffed them, and made a face.

Tomas stripped off his clothes and washed them in the stream first, then set them out to dry. He followed. The icy water stung his skin like thousands of tiny needles, but it drove the last vestiges of his hangover away.

Very few people enjoyed pain, but it sharpened attention

like nothing else. Tomas basked in the sensation. He focused on his breathing and keeping his muscles relaxed.

Still, he could only stay in the stream for a few minutes. He eventually pulled himself out and shook himself dry just as the sun came over the horizon. He lay down next to his clothes, closed his eyes, and let sleep take him.

When he woke, he was warm. Surrounded by tall prairie grasses, the sun beating down on him, he'd sweat as he slept. He squinted and sat up.

Though he'd covered several miles last night, he figured it made more sense to keep resting. He could travel at night and avoid searches. Besides, with the sun warming him, he found he was still tired.

Elzeth chose that moment to make his displeasure known. "What the hell do you think you're doing?"

"Taking a nap."

"You know what I mean."

Tomas' anger flared. "I'm running. Trying to keep us alive, in case you haven't noticed."

Elzeth scoffed. "You call this life?"

"I'm still breathing, so yes."

"I thought we'd left your childishness behind when we came out west."

Elzeth's comment stabbed deep into Tomas' heart, and it cut off his quick and sarcastic retort. He looked down at his palms, as though he'd find answers to his questions written in the lines across his hands. "I did, too."

His sincerity cooled Elzeth's frustration. "We could always go back to Razin."

As foolish as the idea was, the temptation was as strong, and maybe stronger, than it had ever been. Tomas shook his head. "We made the right choice. Besides, you've seen how serious the church is. We'd destroy her life as well as ours."

"Angela might make that sacrifice."

Tomas wanted to believe that was true. He still thought of her, sleeping as he left for the last time. He wore the key to her house around his neck as a constant reminder.

Forgetting her would save him the agony, but he couldn't bring himself to do so. Despite the chaos that had surrounded them, his time with Angela was the only time he could remember where his life had felt right. Like he was living the way he was supposed to.

Leaving had been the correct choice. Anything else was just self-delusion. He'd been proud of himself as he left Razin. Was still proud of himself, in a way. But that choice was like a festering wound, an infection that relentlessly spread through his heart.

The last week had been the worst. Hells, the last day had been the worst. With nothing to do except run, and nothing but time for his mind to wander, he couldn't stop thinking about what could have been.

There was no clean solution. Had she come with him, guilt over forcing Angela to live like this would have eaten him alive. And there was no guarantee their young relationship would have lasted under the strain. But leaving her hadn't been any easier.

Elzeth didn't understand. He'd liked Angela well enough, but his emotions weren't tied up in the affair like Tomas'. His desire to bring the Church to justice for what they'd done outside of Razin consumed him. Instead of running, he wanted to fight.

As a result, Tomas' head hadn't been a pleasant place to dwell. Last night, he'd hoped getting drunk would help. Instead, he'd almost died. Perhaps it was time to give Elzeth's opinions a chance. "I don't suppose you have a suggestion that doesn't end with us suicidally charging some church outpost?"

"We could always *start* by suicidally charging a church outpost."

Tomas snorted. "Seriously, now. Do you really think we should pit ourselves against the church like that?"

Elzeth didn't answer right away, which Tomas appreciated. Even the sagani wasn't that eager to end his life. "I would say," Elzeth started, treading gently, "that we already have. We killed a cardinal, a bunch of knights, and more. But to your point, yes. I think we should. It's time to put something above our own survival."

Tomas sighed. He knew what Elzeth wanted. He just wasn't sure he could give it. "I'll think about it."

Elzeth's frustration bubbled up again, but the sagani tamped it down. This was the first civil conversation they'd had in days, and it wasn't as though the problem was going anywhere.

Tomas lay there, watching the wispy clouds float across the sky. His mind was full of conflicting thoughts, but eventually, he fell asleep.

He woke after nightfall and started walking again. Out here in the prairie, the miles passed quickly underfoot. As far as he could see or hear, he was the only human around, and that was the way he wanted it. If there was any pursuit from the nameless town, they weren't anywhere close.

He picked a direction and followed it, not really caring where his feet took him. His stomach rumbled, not in anger, but in hunger. Fortunately, hunger was an old companion. He could hunt or catch fish. If he got desperate, he could find a farm and either bargain for or steal what little he needed.

As he walked, he considered Elzeth's argument.

The difference between them was that survival was enough for him. All he wanted was to be left in peace. He gazed west. If he just walked far enough in that direction, he'd eventually find a place where no one would bother him.

He grimaced. Comfortable as the familiar thought was, he was starting to realize it wasn't true. Not that there wasn't peace to be found in the isolation of the distant frontier. There was. He just wondered now, if that was what he actually desired.

He would have stayed with Angela. When he'd been forced to flee her home, he hadn't gone west. He might be on the frontier, and he might convince himself that he was better off alone, but he wasn't.

Off in the distance, two sagani prowled for prey. Tomas watched, fascinated. They were about the size of deer, with bodies that almost matched. But their legs were too thick, and the way they prowled the grass made Tomas think more of the leopards in the mountains than deer. "They aren't even coming close to us," he said.

"Saw that. Was wondering why, too."

"You didn't warn them off?" Tomas hadn't felt anything, but he supposed it was possible.

"No. As far as I can tell, they should just think you're a human."

"Curious." Sagani usually had little hesitation about attacking humans.

Tomas watched them for a while longer, but when it was clear they didn't care about him, he continued on.

By the time the sun threatened to rise over the horizon, he'd put many miles between him and the town. His stomach rumbled some more, and Tomas decided when he woke from his next sleep, food would be the first problem he'd tackle.

Except when he woke the next day, it was to an enormous man standing over him, the points of a digging fork held less than an inch from his throat.

3

Tomas slowly raised his hands above his head.

"Don't suppose you were going to wake me up for this?" he asked Elzeth.

"He won't hurt you. Spent five whole minutes debating whether to wake you or leave you alone. He's as gentle as they come."

"He's also a giant. If he sneezes, I'm done for."

"You're fine. Now go make some friends." Elzeth settled back into his customary slumber.

"We are going to have a talk about this."

Elzeth said nothing.

Out loud, Tomas said, "Morning."

"Coming up on afternoon," the giant replied, his voice nearly as deep as he was tall.

"Don't suppose you'd consider kindly removing that digging fork from my throat. It's making me nervous."

The giant lowered the fork until a point rested on Tomas' throat. "Who are you, and what are you doing on my land?"

Tomas studied the man for a moment and took a

gamble. Granted, out here it was usually a pretty safe gamble. "Name's Tomas, and if you need to know, I'm running from the church."

"You forget to tithe last week?"

Tomas grinned. "Something like that."

The giant looked as if he planned to kill Tomas just to spare himself the trouble. Tomas' stomach chose that moment to rumble loudly.

The giant glanced down at Tomas' gut and reconsidered. Then he removed the digging fork from Tomas' throat and extended his hand. "Sorry about the greeting. Strangers aren't too common out here, and I'd prefer to keep my family safe."

"You didn't stab me, so no need to apologize," Tomas said. He took the giant's hand, and the giant lifted him to his feet like he was a child. Hells, next to him, Tomas felt like a child. Standing, he barely reached the man's chest.

The giant shook Tomas' hand. "Name's Nester. My family and I live out here. You're welcome to join us for lunch if you wish."

"I'd be much obliged. Anything I can do in return?"

"There's plenty to go around, and it's no trouble." Nester motioned to Tomas' sword. "I've got a young boy who will probably have a bunch of questions about that. You endure those and don't fill his head with nonsense, and we'll call it even."

Tomas let Nester lead the way. Last night, he didn't have a clue he was close to a farm. When he crested the next rise, the sight brought a smile to his lips. The farm hadn't been more than a quarter-mile away. If he'd kept traveling for another few minutes, he would have walked right into it.

Nester gave him the basic details as they walked. He'd brought his wife and young child out four years ago. They found a plot of land to call their own, built their house, and worked the soil. Though he was modest about the effort, Tomas could imagine what those years had been like. Food had to have been scarce, and supplies hard to come by. Wild sagani would have been a constant threat.

But the effort paid off. Nester's farm was rich in crops, and there were a few livestock grazing nearby. It was almost the life that Tomas imagined for himself.

Nester didn't speak about what had sent him west, and Tomas didn't ask. Everyone had their own reasons for wanting a new start. And Nester had gotten one. It was the promise of the frontier, fulfilled.

A woman stepped out of the house as they neared. She was tall, too, standing an inch or two higher than Tomas. He wondered if the kid would tower over him, too.

When they stepped onto the porch, Nester introduced them. "Tomas, this is my wife, Bertha."

"Pleasure," Tomas said.

Quick footsteps pounded from deeper in the house, and then a young boy burst onto the scene like a tornado tearing across the prairie. The force of nature only stopped when it saw Tomas. He had his father's dark eyes and his mother's gentle expression.

Tomas was just grateful he wasn't the shortest in the house.

Nester grinned from ear to ear. "And this is my son, Radd."

Radd thrust out his hand. "It's an honor to meet you, sir."

Tomas took the proffered hand. "The honor is mine, I assure you."

A grin that was almost a perfect mirror of his father's appeared on Radd's face, and then he was off, tearing across the front yard. Somehow, he'd acquired a long stick while sprinting at full speed, and he was attacking what appeared to be an invading horde of imaginary enemies.

Nester shook his head. "I apologize for any inconvenience he may cause. He's got a good heart, but I don't think he's ever been still for more than a few seconds. Even tosses in his sleep like he's wrestling something."

"It's no problem." Tomas couldn't help but dredge up memories of his own childhood at the sword school. The masters there wouldn't have tolerated such behavior, and they beat stillness into students who needed to learn the skill. As Tomas watched Radd slay yet another imaginary monster, he decided this was the far better childhood.

Nester sighed. "Feel free to relax however you please. Bertha is a fine host, and I've just got to finish up a bit of work before lunch."

"I'd be happy to lend a hand, if you'd like one."

"Oh, there's no need."

"It's the least I can do, given the promise of food."

Nester relented, and that was how Tomas found himself pulling potatoes from the garden. It wasn't the sort of task he performed often, but once he found the rhythm, he discovered harvesting was almost as meditative as running through his sword forms.

Between the two adults and Radd, they quickly finished the task. Tomas helped Nester haul the potatoes back to the house, and his mouth watered as the scents of Bertha's cooking wafted out the front door.

They washed up and sat at the table, enormous bowls of stew and fresh baked bread waiting for them. It was the feast of Tomas' dreams, and it took all his control not to devour every scrap of food on his plate and everyone else's.

From the amused looks Nester exchanged with Bertha, he wasn't controlling himself as well as he thought.

When the meal ended, Tomas thanked Bertha. "I can honestly say that was one of the most delicious meals I've ever eaten."

She beamed.

"Thank you, again, for the hospitality," Tomas said. "It's meant a lot to me."

Nester and Bertha exchanged another look, engaging in that silent conversation that reminded Tomas so much of the way he and Elzeth spoke to one another. She gave a small nod.

"You don't have to leave right away," Nester said. "We'd be happy to let you rest here for a few days."

Tomas didn't think long on the proposal. He was tired and he liked the family. Bertha's cooking sealed the deal.

"Thank you. I'd like that very much."

4

Tomas spent the next three days living a life close to the one he'd so long desired. While Nester's house wasn't quite as isolated as the house of Tomas' dreams, it was still miles from the nearest neighbor.

The family woke before the rising of the sun, for daylight was their most precious resource. They broke their fast with Bertha's simple but filling meals, and then Tomas, Radd, and Nester worked the fields. Winter approached, and the family raced against the season to finish the harvest. Tomas suspected this was no small part of the reason they had invited him in. Even with his help, there was no telling if they would beat the killing frosts. Every morning they woke with bated breath, wondering if the overnight temperature had dropped low enough to destroy what crop remained.

Tomas kept a wary eye on the horizon. But as the days passed, his worry eased. He wasn't naïve enough to believe that he was safe, but he figured it would be several days before the search found him here. He'd repay Nester's kindness as well as he was able, then take his leave.

While his body labored, his mind wandered. He considered Elzeth's arguments, but any conclusive answer remained elusive. Sure, he wanted to make the church suffer, but doing so risked everything. He enjoyed wandering the frontier and meeting families like Nester's. Though his body ached after a day in the fields, he found he preferred picking potatoes to picking up his sword.

He might not be changing the world, but why was that his responsibility?

Anyway, proud as he was, he wasn't so foolish as to believe he could hurt the church in any meaningful way. It was rich, expansive, and had thousands upon thousands of people who believed in it so strongly they would lay down their lives for it. He couldn't fight against that, no more than he could stop the seasons from turning.

Though he didn't reach a decision, he enjoyed a temporary truce with Elzeth. The sagani liked Nester's family and was grateful that Tomas was doing something with his time more productive than drinking himself into oblivion. They spoke little, but Tomas felt the sagani's mood lift a little higher with each day they spent in the fields.

On the evening of the third day, Nester pulled out a jug of wine. He poured for each of the adults, and they toasted the harvest as they finished their meal.

As Bertha went about the process that ended, hopefully, with Radd passed out in his bed, Nester and Tomas went to the porch and sat in the chairs Nester had made himself. Nester poured him another cup of wine, and they drank as they watched Tolkin rise.

"I take it you'll be leaving once the harvest is done?" Nester asked.

Tomas nodded.

"You could settle here, if you wanted." Nester gestured to

the endless expanse of grassland beyond their house. "Plenty of space, and I don't think I'd mind having you for a neighbor. Might even help you build a home, if you ask nice enough."

Tomas chuckled. "A tempting offer. Truly."

"Not one for staying in place?"

Tomas twirled the wine gently around the inside of his cup. He supposed it wouldn't hurt Nester to know a bit more about the guest he was in danger of calling a friend. "No. I've long dreamed of settling. But it would be dangerous. Eventually, someone would find me."

"Your enemies are that determined?"

"They are."

"I've heard it said you can judge a man by the quality of his enemies."

Tomas laughed out loud at that. "If that's true, I'm either the greatest of heroes or the worst of villains. Depending on who you ask, I suppose."

"Hard to believe."

Maybe it was the wine, or maybe Tomas just trusted the giant man. "I've made enemies of both the Family and the church, and they've even paid off the marshals to hunt me down."

He expected Nester to kick him out of the house at that confession. Any sane man would have done so.

He certainly didn't expect the giant to laugh so loud he could feel it in his bones. "You speak true?"

"I do."

"You must tell me how!"

Tomas frowned. "Sure you don't want me to leave?"

"Ha! I'd ask you to build your house closer." At Tomas' questioning glance, he explained. "There's no love lost in this house for either the church or the Family. So, how did this come about?"

"Never liked either, myself," Tomas said. "A while back, I encouraged the Family and church to go to war over a town. Ended up burning down the town."

Nester laughed again. Tomas hadn't guessed the giant possessed such mirth.

"Then I kept bumping into the church and causing problems for them. Ended up killing a cardinal who was running some experiments on children."

Nester's good cheer died at that. "Is that so?"

Tomas nodded. "So, while I appreciate the offer, it's best that I leave before someone finds me. I have no wish to bring any harm to you or your family."

Nester thought for a moment. "It's an unfair world that punishes those who do good. Want to know why we settled all the way out here?"

Tomas admitted that he'd been curious.

"Bertha grew up a believer in the church. I never was, but saw no harm in following her ways. We were married in the church and tithed honestly. Back before all this, I was a soldier in the army, and gone for long stretches. I couldn't wait for my term of enlistment to end. Radd had just been born, and I looked forward to becoming the father he deserves. But work was hard to find. The best work went to those associated with the Family in town, and most of the rest to the church. I talked to the local priest and asked if the church might help us. He offered me the opportunity to become a knight."

Nester finished his wine and refilled both their cups. "That presented a bit of a problem. I enjoyed being home, being a real father. Besides, Bertha was the believer, not me. I figured I was done laying my life down for other people's causes. Bertha and I talked about it, and we decided against it. I told the priest I was honored by the invitation, but it wasn't for me."

The giant man stared out into the fields, but saw only the past. "Things changed after that. Supplies and food became expensive. Fewer people talked to us at church. What little work I had found evaporated. One time, the priest spoke with us and reminded me that his offer was still available. Eventually, we had to stop donating to the church, because there wasn't enough money for both us and it. Members became downright vicious toward us. One day, I realized I either had to borrow money from the Family or leave."

"I'm sorry," Tomas said.

"Don't be. Leaving was the best decision this family ever made. Life isn't easy out here, but I get to see Radd every day. Bertha and I are closer than ever. Coming out west is a decision I should have made long before I did."

Tomas blamed the wine for loosening his tongue. "I left a woman back in the town where I killed the cardinal."

"She didn't want to run?"

"She would have, I think. Said she would, at least. But she was the marshal in town. A good one, too. I couldn't ask her to run, couldn't ask her to leave what she'd built."

"Regret it?"

"Every day. But I'm not sure what else I could have done."

Nester rubbed his chin. "I'm not sure what to tell you. Your problems are greater than the ones I faced. But I can tell you this: I'd rather be on the run, sharing the dangers with my family, than separated from them."

He held out his hand, and Tomas put his empty cup in it. "Thanks."

"You're very welcome. Just know, you ever do decide to settle down, that offer of being our neighbor stands."

"I appreciate that."

They returned to the house, where Bertha had finally won the war that ended with Radd asleep in bed. Tomas went to the guest room, leaving the couple some time alone. Another day or two of harvesting, and then he'd be off.

He fell asleep quickly that night.

But woke soon after. Elzeth stirred him awake.

"Someone's approaching," he said.

5

The footsteps' owner tried hard to be quiet, but Elzeth wasn't so easily deceived. Tomas groaned and cracked one eye open. The footsteps stopped outside his door, and the knob slowly turned. The door opened and a small face appeared in the slit.

Radd waited a moment, then opened the door the rest of the way. He crept into Tomas' room, placing his feet carefully. The boy apparently knew where every creaky plank was. He fixed his eyes on Tomas' sword, resting in the corner. He rubbed his hands together in silent anticipation.

At Tomas' unspoken request, Elzeth sharpened his hearing. In the room adjacent, Nester stirred and his breathing quickened. Radd's attempts to sneak through the house had not gone unnoticed. His poor host was probably torn between barging in and waiting to see what Radd did.

Tomas let the boy get within a step of his sword before clearing his throat. "Don't see swords often?"

Radd jumped almost a foot off the ground, yelping in surprise. Through the walls, Tomas heard Nester chuckling.

"I'm sorry, sir!" Radd looked to be on the verge of a

very long and most likely convoluted apology. Tomas cut it off by standing and walking over to his sword. He picked it up and handed it to Radd. "Here. Take a look."

The boy's eyes went wide. "Do you mean it?"

"If it means I can sleep through the night without you sneaking into my room again, yes."

Radd's cheeks turned crimson, but he soon forgot his shame as fascination consumed him. "May I?"

"Sure."

Radd drew the blade a few inches from the sheath. "Is it sharp?"

"Very."

Tomas could see the boy wanted desperately to touch the edge, but was pleased to see he had the good sense not to. Eventually, he slid the blade all the way back into the sheath. His gaze turned up toward Tomas. "Will you teach me?"

"No. I'll be leaving in a day or two, and that's something your father should do, anyhow."

Radd frowned. "Dad doesn't fight. He won't even argue in town over prices the way Mom thinks he should."

Tomas heard a snort of Bertha's laughter from the next room. "Your father has the right of it, at least regarding weapons."

"But you fight people, don't you?"

And this, Tomas decided, was why he planned on never having children. Too many questions. He sighed. Neither Nester nor Bertha seemed to be in any hurry to help him out. "Yes, I fight. And sometimes, people should. But I rarely want to."

Radd's expression changed. He didn't look so interested in Tomas anymore. He handed the sword back, then remembered his manners. "Thanks for letting me look. Sorry I came into your room."

Tomas let him go without further warnings, and from the sounds of it, Nester and Bertha intended to do the same.

This time, when he fell asleep, no one bothered him.

THE NEXT EVENING, they were just finishing the harvest as the sun fell below the horizon. Tomas figured he'd stay one last night, then get an early start in the morning. Though he had seen no one since he arrived, he'd intruded on Nester's hospitality long enough.

"Thanks for last night," Nester said as Tomas picked up another full basket of food.

"You're welcome. I'm afraid Radd no longer looks at me as a great hero."

"He's young and knows that I served in the military. It makes sense that he's enamored with weapons."

"You think you'll train him?"

"Everything I know, once I'm certain he's old enough to handle the responsibility. Out here, he'll need the skills."

"Agreed. He's a good kid, though."

"Except for when he runs off on one of his adventures," Nester said. "He should have been back here in time to help us finish."

Tomas frowned. He'd been so lost in that now-familiar meditative trance of harvesting that he hadn't even been paying attention. "Have you seen him recently?" he asked Elzeth.

"No."

He shrugged and helped Nester carry the final bits of the harvest to the house. Inside, Bertha was hard at work, making a late supper and organizing the harvest for her preparations the next day. "Radd in here?" Nester asked his wife.

She hadn't seen him, either. Nester sighed. "I'll go check his room. Sometimes he sneaks in to hide from the chores."

Elzeth sharpened Tomas' hearing, but even with it, Tomas couldn't hear anyone in the house besides the three adults. He said nothing, though. Nester would find out in a minute, and Tomas had no desire to reveal that he was a host.

He stepped outside and circled around the house. As far as he'd seen, Radd almost always remained nearby, in sight of either Nester or Bertha. But he couldn't see any signs of the boy. He heard nothing, either.

A small knot of worry settled in the pit of his stomach. There were a dozen explanations, of course, but a handful of those frightened him.

Nester emerged from the house about the same time that Tomas finished circling it. "He's not in there," the giant said.

"I didn't see him anywhere outside, either."

"Fool boy. Probably fell asleep in the grass somewhere, tired from all his antics last night."

If that was the explanation, Tomas would have been relieved. "You should let me look for him."

Nester waved his concern away. "Nonsense. We can search together."

Tomas caught him by the wrist as Nester walked away. "Nester. It might be best to stay near Bertha, at least for a bit. If he has fallen asleep somewhere out here, I can find him fast. You have my word."

Nester's nostrils flared. He and Tomas hadn't known each other long, and Tomas knew he asked for a significant amount of trust. "Fine," he said. "See if you can find him. If he's wandered off, it's most likely west. There's a stream there he enjoys playing around."

Tomas nodded, thankful the big man would stay in place. He was even more grateful that he'd earned his host's trust.

Without another word, they separated. Nester went to keep watch with Bertha, and Tomas searched for the missing boy.

Nester's advice was as good a place as any to start. If the boy wasn't by the stream, Tomas would circle around. It hadn't rained since Tomas had arrived at Nester's place. That had been excellent for the family as they'd finished bringing in the harvest, but it meant that tracking Radd's light footsteps would be a challenge.

Tomas wandered west, following a random, serpentine route. Elzeth burned gently, alert for any dangers.

His heightened senses failed to pick up any sign of the boy. The uneasiness in his stomach grew. He'd only been with the family for a bit, and Radd certainly suffered from the typical difficulties associated with being an active and curious boy, but the child had never struck Tomas as being irresponsible. Out here, with the sagani roaming around, carelessness wasn't a luxury afforded to many.

Before long, he heard the soft sounds of a creek. He continued weaving back and forth, covering as much ground as he could. He reached the creek a few minutes later.

It wasn't much of a creek. This late in the season, the water looked to be about half as high as it would be during the height of the spring snowmelt. Its surface was smooth, reflecting Tolkin's image at Tomas' feet.

A small grove of trees stood farther north, and Tomas had a hunch he would find Radd's hideout there. The combination of trees and water would be irresistible for a child.

As he approached the grove, Tomas grew more cautious. He crouched down and walked low. The night was almost cloudless, and Tolkin provided more than enough light to see by. It aided his search, but if the worst had come to pass, and there were enemies out here, it made him plenty visible, too. Still, his eyes, ears, and nose all told him he was alone.

He reached the edge of the trees and still heard nothing. The knot in his stomach pulled tighter. This close, he should have been able to hear Radd's breathing.

He stepped into the grove, grateful for the small amount of protection the trees provided. Tonight would be a wonderful night for a sniper.

He searched the grove and found Radd's hideout. Small, whittled figurines rested around a patch of ground that had been well trampled. Tomas looked around and decided that he liked Radd's taste in hideouts. The place was hidden from the house. The trees provided plenty of shade and shelter, and there was a little bend in the stream just ahead that Tomas suspected provided excellent fishing.

Tomas followed the well-worn trail to the stream and stopped. He crouched down and picked up a piece of fabric that had caught his eye. It was just a small scrap, but it was from the shirt Radd had been wearing that day. Tomas took a step back and took in the entire scene.

There could have been a struggle here, though Tomas wasn't sure. The area was too well traveled. A wide trail of broken grasses led across the stream and farther west. Tomas took a running start and jumped across the water.

Here, on the other side, the evidence was clearer. The jump was at the edges of Tomas' unaided ability. Radd hadn't been able to make it, but the stream was plenty low enough to walk across. Tomas found one small set of footprints in the mud, accompanied by two larger sets.

He swore. A smarter man would have left Nester's right after that first meal. He'd liked the giant, though, and had clearly been desperate for company. That neediness had put the family at risk.

"You should be madder at the scum that kidnapped the child," Elzeth said.

"We should have left."

"No. You stayed to enjoy Nester's company and to help with their harvest. If you blame yourself for even that, you'll be digging yourself into a hole you'll never climb out of."

Tomas growled, deep in his throat.

He looked back to where Nester's house stood. The giant deserved to know what had happened to his son.

Tomas shook his head. True as the sentiment might be, time was valuable, and there was little to be gained by running back. Once, Nester might have been a skilled warrior, but he was years out of practice. Easier to do this on his own.

He turned and followed the trail. Despite the dry conditions, he found it an effortless task. The kidnappers and Radd had walked abreast of one another, making no effort to disguise their escape.

Either he was up against poorly trained kidnappers, or they were deliberately leaving a trail. He could have followed their path with one eye closed.

The tracks aimed straight for another small clump of trees, perhaps a half-mile away. Tomas dropped into a resting squat, leaving the top of his head just above the prairie grasses. He focused on the trees and waited.

It didn't take long. They were smart enough at least not to have lit a fire, but shadows moved within the trees. He expanded his search, looking for sentries or outlooks, but saw nothing. Though he couldn't be sure, it didn't seem like there were more than three or four people in the trees.

The scene didn't sit right with him.

Wasn't much he could do about it, though. If Radd was in there, it was where he needed to go. Another downside to liking people, he supposed.

He debated his approach for a minute, then stood up. He walked straight for the grove of trees.

The closer he got, the more he could discern. There were three people in the small grove. One sat on a downed log, with the other two behind him. An adult held Radd close. He still couldn't see their faces, hidden in the shadows of the trees as they were.

The man holding Radd told Tomas to stop about thirty paces away from the group. Tomas obeyed. He saw the glint of metal near Radd's throat and had no problem imagining the blade pressed tight there.

"Be ready, Elzeth."

The sagani burned brighter in response.

Tomas still couldn't see into the shadows. He knew the figures were there, but their faces remained stubbornly elusive. It made it difficult to guess their exact intent.

He looked around, but as near as he could tell, they were alone. Did they not know he was a host? If he could just get a little closer, or create some sort of opening, he could reach Radd's captor before he could act.

His hopes died when the man sitting on the log spoke. Tomas startled as he heard a ghost from the past speak his name.

"Tomas, old friend, it's been far, far too long."

6

The voice turned Tomas' insides to water.

Not because the man physically threatened him. Tomas had nothing to fear if they dueled.

No, what frightened Tomas was what the man represented. They certainly weren't as alone as Tomas had hoped. He kept his voice light, a feat considering the circumstances. "Hux. It's been a long time. Though I must admit, not long enough."

Hux grunted. "You always were the witty one. Only thing faster than your sword was your tongue. That's what I used to say about you. Seems like the years haven't seen fit to bless us all with your silence."

"If you didn't want to listen to me, there are an awful lot of other places you could be."

Hux shook his head. "Of all the places in the world, there's nowhere else I'd rather be right now."

Tomas' eyes darted around the horizon, but he still didn't see anyone, and that made him terribly uncomfortable. Hux always kept at least one rifle in the gang.

"You've been busy since I saw you last," Hux said, enjoying Tomas' discomfort. "You've somehow become the only person wanted either dead or alive by both the church and the Family. Why, you've become the only thing they agree on!"

"Always considered myself something of a peacemaker," Tomas said, still searching for the threats he was sure were near. As long as Hux was talking, Radd kept breathing. So, in that sense, at least, Tomas was winning. The biggest downside was he had to keep listening to Hux. "Why are you here, Hux? Why now?"

Hux held up a pair of steel manacles. "Found a new boss. Or rather, a new boss found us. Quite the fella, if you ask me. But he says he prefers you alive, and given that you and we have a bit of a history, he thought we might just be the only ones who could talk you into willingly putting on these here manacles and coming all peaceably."

"You forget to tell your new boss we didn't part on the best of terms?"

"Oh, he seemed to know enough about that. He still reckoned our powers of persuasion might just be sufficient."

"Where are the others?"

A grin lit Hux's face, his teeth visible in the moonlight. "Oh, they're around. You'll remember a few of them. Others are new, but I think you'll be impressed. It's gotten harder to be an honest outlaw these days. Those still in the life have to be strong to survive." Hux spit. "Now, enough jawing. You going to put these on, or do we have to kill the kid?"

"You kill the kid and your life is forfeit."

Tomas' threat didn't seem to bother Hux in the least. Which worried Tomas. Hux, more than most, knew exactly what Tomas was capable of. Hux pulled out a pocket watch. "Figured you might say something like that." He held up the watch. "You want to know where the others are? They're surrounding the house you've been hiding in the past week. If they don't get the signal from me soon, they'll burn the house down, including the two in it."

Hux put the pocket watch away. "Now, I know for a fact you're bluffing about the boy. Even at your meanest, you were never one to harm children. But I have an even harder time believing you'd sacrifice an entire innocent family." He held up the manacles. "Hells, I can even guess what you're thinking right now. You're thinking the gang never was that smart, and that maybe you can let yourself get captured and make an escape."

Tomas grimaced. His thoughts had been wandering in that direction.

Hux shrugged. "Maybe you're right. I'll admit I've got a few young'ins working under me that might get lax. But I'll tell you this: surrendering is the only way you'll save this family. Otherwise, someone's going to die tonight."

Tomas' mind raced.

"Tick, tock," Hux said. "Sorry, but I can't give you too much time to decide. We'd expected you'd track us down faster. You're slowing down in your old age."

"What guarantee do I have you won't hurt them after I surrender?"

Hux laughed. "Don't be a child, Tomas. You have none. Except that it is not in my best interests for you to be more angry than necessary at me, and I bear no ill will against the family. You know I admire the frontier spirit."

Tomas cursed to himself. Hux had always been too clever for his own good.

Just as he was about to hold out his hands for Hux to toss the manacles to him, Radd took Tomas' decision away.

He'd stood through the entire exchange, perfectly still. Now he stomped down hard on his captor's foot.

For just a heartbeat, the man's grip failed in surprise. Radd, quick as he was, sprinted away, hopping over logs like an oversized jackrabbit.

Tomas didn't hesitate. He leaped forward, Elzeth burning bright as the sun. They stopped short of unity, but not by much. He covered the thirty paces between them in two heartbeats. He went after Radd's captor, as the man was considerably closer to the child than Hux.

Radd's captor twisted toward Radd, intending to chase after the boy and secure him again. That motion took away whatever slight chance he might have had against the host. Tomas drew his sword and beheaded the man in one elegant motion. He slid to a stop and leaped toward Hux, who was already on his feet.

For the first time that night, he got a clear view of the man who had once led the gang Tomas had been proud to be part of. Tolkin's light illuminated every part of his face, and it was sickeningly familiar.

Too familiar. It had been years since Tomas and Hux had parted ways, but it looked like he had barely aged a day.

Then Hux drew his own sword, and their blades crossed.

With Elzeth burning as bright as he was, Hux shouldn't have had a chance. But his parry of Tomas' cut was perfect.

Tomas finally solved the last part of the mystery, the question that had been troubling him since he learned it was Hux setting the trap. Why had Hux been willing to risk dueling Tomas with so few people nearby?

It was because he'd become a host, too.

7

Tomas' surprise only disoriented him for a moment, but Hux was determined to milk that moment for all it was worth. He launched an impressive series of lightning-quick cuts.

Hux advanced relentlessly, his sword never pausing. Already off-balance, Tomas had little choice but to retreat. He stepped back, using the time to study his former boss.

Even for a host, Hux seemed fast. Elzeth burned brightly, and Hux was almost as fast as Tomas.

When Hux snarled and gnashed his teeth, his eyes wild, Tomas understood. Hux hadn't just become a host.

He was a host teetering on the edge of madness. The more he burned, the closer he came to losing all reason. And the strongest hosts were those walking the razor's edge of insanity.

Eventually, Hux launched himself at Tomas. It was a poorly considered move, and Tomas had little trouble stepping out of the way and cutting Hux as he passed. It was nothing more than a scratch, but Hux gave no sign he'd just been cut.

Even more telling, for almost half a minute after, Hux kept swinging at empty air. Tomas kept away, content to watch. He heard Radd breathing heavy behind a nearby tree. Hux's madness fascinated the boy, too.

Hux stopped swinging his sword and looked around, his confusion evident. Then he turned, saw Tomas, and howled.

Had his effort cost Hux his last scraps of reason? When Hux licked his blade, cutting his own tongue, Tomas decided the answer was yes.

It had been a while since he'd come across a host near the end of their life. The sight disgusted him, and yet he couldn't help but feel pity for his former boss. The man had done nothing in life that earned him the slightest bit of mercy, but somehow, the madness of a host still seemed too cruel a fate.

And the thought lurked, always in the back of Tomas' mind, that a similar future awaited him. He'd held it off far longer than most, and he still hoped there was some chance he might somehow avoid his fate, but he wasn't holding his breath.

Hosts went mad. He was a host. The conclusion was inescapable.

If he somehow lived that long, he hoped that someone would grant him the same courtesy he was about to extend to Hux.

Hux charged, his sword carving wild arcs in the rapidly diminishing space between them. He gave no thought to defense, and it was easy enough to find an opening. Tomas stepped into one and gave Hux a far cleaner death than he deserved.

The body fell, finally at rest. Despite his personal hatred for the man, Tomas still said the old words over him. As he did, he heard Radd emerge from behind the tree. The boy didn't step toward him, though.

Tomas cleaned his sword and sheathed it. The appearance of Hux had flung his thoughts far into the past. Though they'd just crossed swords, he struggled to believe the body in front of him was real.

When the two of them had first crossed paths, Tomas had been a very different man. A very broken man. One that Hux had seen, correctly, as an opportunity.

Tomas had strength, but after the war, no purpose. Hux, who had also fought for the losing side, had a simple plan: take from the victors until there was nothing left to take. Their hate was pure, and Hux's charisma and cleverness attracted a competent assortment of criminals.

Tomas ran with them for about a year. They robbed banks, stagecoaches, and more. Though he never wished to return to those times, they remained vivid in his memories and dreams.

Mostly because of her. The ghost that haunted him more than any of the others.

"I can't believe he became a host," Elzeth said. "He hated the idea."

Tomas nodded. He'd wondered, briefly, if Hux had become a host just for this encounter. But that couldn't be true. Hux's movements had shown none of the compensations new hosts used to adjust to their sudden increase in strength and speed. And the madness had been well developed. No, Hux had been a host for years.

Any answers would be with the others.

Tomas took one last look at his old boss. If Hux had a weakness, it was the confidence in his own plans. When he was right, it made him almost unstoppable. They'd pulled off heists no one had even considered possible.

And with madness consuming Hux, he was faster and stronger than Tomas had been in the past. Hux had planned tonight well, but he'd been too confident. And he'd underestimated the boy.

The thought of Radd made Tomas look around. The boy was nowhere to be found. "Where'd he go?"

He feared he already knew the answer.

"Ran back to the house," Elzeth said. "Sorry, I thought you noticed."

"A bit distracted here. How long ago?"

"Few minutes."

Tomas swore and sprinted after the boy. Hux hadn't been lying about the others, and he didn't want to rescue Radd a second time today.

When he was about halfway to the house, he slowed. He saw Radd's head, several hundred yards ahead, about to reach the house. The boy had too much of a lead, and Tomas had no chance of catching him in time. He found a clump of tall grasses he could hide behind and watched.

Radd ran into the house, his progress unchecked by anyone watching the building.

Had Hux been bluffing?

No, he hadn't. There, in the grass between Tomas and Nester's home, was movement. A head poked above the grass and looked around.

It wasn't anyone Tomas recognized, but that wasn't surprising. Hux's line of work didn't promote longevity, and it had been many years since Tomas had seen any of them. If Hux had more than one or two members of the original gang together, Tomas would have been shocked.

If Nester and Bertha hadn't known their house was surrounded, they would with Radd's arrival.

Tomas couldn't guess how they would react, but he didn't want to give them enough time to decide.

He crawled to where he'd seen the man in the grass. He heard the man shift his weight frequently. Tomas didn't raise his own head to confirm, but he guessed the man was constantly poking his head up, looking for threats like a gopher popping its head out of a hole.

For all the man's vigilance, he never saw Tomas coming. He was loud enough he couldn't hear the slight sounds of Tomas' approach. When Tomas burst from a nearby clump and killed him with a knife, the man never responded.

Before Tomas could scout the area more completely, he heard footsteps, inhumanly fast.

And they were running straight for him.

8

Whoever approached, they knew where he was, so there was little point in hiding. He stood, drawing his sword as he turned. His eyes opened wide when he saw who it was, and the tip of his sword dropped.

She was the ghost of a hundred nightmares, the sum of his greatest regrets.

She swung her sword with incredible speed, and he blocked poorly. Steel met steel, ringing across the moonlit plains. The impact knocked Tomas back, and his feet danced quickly to keep him upright.

She didn't speak. Her sword said plenty, and it kept trying to carve his heart out of his chest. He blocked and retreated, always a step behind. Part of his mind refused to believe this was real. Had madness overtaken his reason?

There was nothing imaginary about the way her sword whispered through the tall grass. He didn't doubt the power of her strikes as the hilt of his sword vibrated in his hands.

She had also become a host. She'd always been a skilled sword, but this speed was impossible for a human. Besides, her face was almost exactly as he remembered it, which meant she had become a host not long after he'd left her to die. Just like Hux.

An arrow whistled through the air behind Tomas, and he risked glancing to the side. Two archers had emerged from the grass. One was nocking another arrow, while the other held her aim steady on the duel. Tomas kept closer to his assailant.

No point in giving the archers an easy shot.

Other footsteps rushed to join the battle, and Tomas soon faced four swords in addition to the two archers. Only she was a host, but it was enough.

Under other circumstances, Tomas was certain he would have emerged triumphant. He spotted plenty of openings, and Tomas could have whittled their numbers down.

But her presence unbalanced him. He dodged, but not as fast as he should have. He cut without wanting to strike. Though he was a host, they maintained the advantage.

He didn't want to hurt her again.

Unfortunately, she had no such hesitation.

She had always been tempestuous, laughing gaily one moment and fighting with all her heart the next. When he'd been younger and lost in a world he barely understood, clinging to her had been the adventure of a lifetime. One he still thought of, frequently. When he was with her, he'd been the stable one, his feet and thoughts rooted deeply in reality.

He'd needed that.

Tonight, she unleashed the full power of her fury upon him, and he had no will to resist.

Their blades crossed again, and again, he stumbled backward. He surrendered to gravity when he noticed the archers grinning from ear to ear. Their arrows split the air overhead as he fell back. He rolled over his shoulder and back to his feet, just in time to meet the four swords cutting down at him.

Tomas needed to find his will to live. But that will, which he'd relied on so many times in the past few years, was nowhere to be found.

If anyone had a right to kill him, it was her. Hells, it was almost criminal to deny her the chance.

He defended, but the longer he fought, the more her presence sapped his strength.

The swords drove him back, and the archers moved with the group, keeping their sight lines open. All it would take was one mistake too many, and he'd be too far gone to recover. He couldn't bring himself to care.

Then one archer collapsed, the movement catching everyone by surprise. A heartbeat later, before the second one could react, she fell, too. An arrow had punched clean through the side of her skull.

Two of the swords turned. Tomas struck out at them, but she was there, more than capable of defending the others.

"Go!" Her shout almost forced Tomas to his knees. Once, she had held such power over him.

The third sword joined the others, leaving her and Tomas alone. He looked over her shoulder and saw Nester and Bertha standing together, with little Radd behind them. Both adults carried bows, Nester's looking too big for human hands.

As Tomas watched, Nester drew his enormous bow and released. The gang was moving, but Nester never hesitated. The arrow flew so fast that even Tomas, with Elzeth burning brightly, could barely see it. It punched one swordsman in the chest, exiting out his back without seeming to slow at all.

The sight of Nester and Bertha defending their home and family lit the fire in his heart that self-preservation couldn't. Where she was concerned, he cared little about his life. But he wouldn't leave Nester and Bertha to fight against her alone.

She swung at him again, strong as ever. He parried the cut, his feet digging firmly into the dirt. Then he countered.

For the first time that night, she had no choice but to retreat. She kicked dirt at his face as he pursued.

Tomas closed his eyes as he shuffled to the side.

Their battle began in earnest.

He was faster and was still the better sword. He always had been, even without Elzeth.

But she possessed a remarkable ability that reminded him of the various "drunken" martial schools that sometimes rose to prominence. Her movements were too chaotic to predict, and she used the environment in creative ways no one ever expected. Combined with her skill with a blade, she was a fearsome opponent for any fighter.

Now he saw the full extent of her ability. Clean as his cuts were, they always missed. She was never quite where he expected her to be, and her movements were never exactly what he predicted.

She rolled once, when there was no need to roll, but she came up with a handful of dirt that she tossed at his face. Another time, she let him past her guard, only to have his cut blocked by vambraces she wore under her sleeves.

He'd forgotten about those.

Despite his difficulties, he was winning. Now that the surprise of her presence had worn off, the difference in their skill became apparent. She might avoid his cuts, but that was far different from beating him. She never would concede, but it was in her best interests.

When the fight ended, it wasn't because of something either of them did.

An arrow punched through her left shoulder, narrowly missing Tomas as it flew clean through. The blow spun her around, and by the time she was facing Tomas again, he had reversed the grip on his sword. He drove the bottom of the hilt up at her chin. The hilt connected solidly, and her eyes rolled up in her head.

She collapsed to the ground, and Tomas breathed a sigh of relief. His senses told him the rest of the gang was dead. The family was safe.

Now, though, he had to explain to a very angry giant why he'd brought such danger to his doorstep.

Tomas gulped and looked down at her unconscious form.

Maybe he should have let her kill him, after all.

9

Tomas' first task was to bind her. Despite her wounds, he didn't think she'd be unconscious for long. Her sagani would keep her under for as little time as possible. Fortunately, Tomas found another pair of manacles in one of her pockets. She'd been Hux's ace in the hole. He locked her hands behind her back and pocketed the key.

Satisfied that he was in no immediate danger, he looked toward Nester and his family. Bertha had already unstrung her bow and was escorting Radd back into the house. The boy looked as though she was taking candy away from him. Far from teaching him the dangers of violence, the night had only seemed to whet his appetite. But Tomas trusted Nester would use the night's events to teach Radd well.

Everyone else around the house was dead. Nester and Bertha's arrows had destroyed the enemy.

"First time I've seen a battlefield where you weren't the one responsible for most of the bodies," Elzeth said.

"I was busy with her!" Tomas protested.

Elzeth snorted and settled into a watchful wariness. He

could light again in a moment if Tomas needed him. But with the primary danger past, he would rest.

The greatest danger, as near as Tomas could tell, was Nester putting one of those oversized arrows through him. He sheathed his blade and looked at the giant farmer.

Nester didn't unstring his bow. He still had an arrow nocked, and he approached Tomas as though he approached an enemy. When he was close enough to speak at a normal volume, he stopped. "You a host?"

"I am."

"You going mad?"

"Not as far as I can tell. But you've been with me for a week. Have I shown any tics that concern you?"

The point of the arrow dropped a bit. "What are you planning next?"

Tomas looked down at the unconscious woman at his feet. "I was already planning on leaving tomorrow. But now it looks like I need to leave even earlier. Seems I have more enemies than I thought."

"Thought it was already a pretty extensive list."

Tomas chuckled. "I suppose it was. I talked to the boss of the group before I killed him. Someone hired them to find me, and I suspect that person won't stop until I find them and have a bit of a sit-down." Tomas met Nester's gaze. "I'm sorry I put your family in danger. It was never my intent."

The point of the arrow dropped to the ground, and Nester relaxed his grip on the bowstring. "You were honest enough about the forces coming after you. Nothing here for you to regret."

Tomas gestured to the bow, hoping to mask the sudden surge of emotion that hit him with Nester's forgiveness. "Quite the weapon you've got there. I don't think I've ever seen one quite like it."

Nester's grin stretched from ear to ear. "Yeah. Radd's always disappointed I wasn't a swordsman, but I grew up with a bow in my hands, and it's always been my preferred weapon. Never could get used to a sword."

"Well, you saved me tonight. And gave me food and shelter for a week, so I've got nothing but gratitude. Is there anything I can do for you before I leave? Move the bodies?"

Nester shook his head. "We'll bury them tomorrow. I think it'll be good for Radd to see the consequences, and they'll make an excellent fertilizer for the garden. She's not dead, though."

"I know. Need to talk to her about what happened here."

Nester gave him a knowing look. "You two have history?"

"I ran with them many years ago."

Nester shook his head. "I hope my life is never as interesting as yours, no offense."

"None taken."

"We've got a spare pack and plenty of food. Bertha can fill it for you before you leave."

Tomas looked to the sky, trying to get a sense of how much time was left in the night. "I really should be going."

"Won't take but a few minutes, and it'll give you a chance to say goodbye to the others."

There was something about the simple kindness he couldn't refuse. "Fair enough." Before he followed Nester, he drew a knife from his belt and stabbed the woman in the stomach.

When Nester frowned, he explained. "She's a host. The sagani inside her will keep her asleep while she's healing, and she'll be a lot easier to move if she isn't fighting."

They returned to the house together and found Bertha and Radd already loading the spare pack, as though they'd come to the same conclusion as Nester. Tomas said his goodbyes, thanking them profusely for all the aid they'd given him. A few minutes later, as Nester had promised, he was out on the front deck, wondering which way to go.

Nester stood beside him. "You want to avoid company, west is your best choice. There are other farms out there, but they're few and far between. No towns for several days, at least."

"Thanks again," Tomas said. "If there's ever anything I can do for you, all you have to do is ask."

Nester waved his offer away. "If you ever find your life too exciting and want to escape it, come on back. My offer of helping you build a place still stands, provided you don't have hosts coming to kill you every week. I've got a feeling you've got some stories that would make the nights pass an awful lot faster."

"That I do." Tomas bowed, said his thanks once again, and took his leave of the house.

He found her right where he'd left her. The wound in her stomach was already closed, the scar barely visible.

"What do you think?" he asked Elzeth. "Keep her out?"

"Even with me, you're not going to carry her for that long," Elzeth said. "Take her weapons and let her wake up when she wakes up. So long as she's manacled, there's not much she can do to us."

As usual, the sagani spoke sense, and so Tomas ran his hands up and down her body. He felt dirty doing it, but if he remembered anything, it was how fond she was of hiding weapons in places both reasonable and not. Sure enough, by the time he was done, he'd found a fair number of knives, needles, lock picks, and other sharp objects. He bundled them up and stuffed them in the pack. Not that she wasn't already trying to kill him, but she'd be even more eager if he left her weapons behind. He tied her sword to his right hip, then heaved her up and over his shoulder.

She was lighter than he remembered. With Elzeth's assistance, her weight was barely an inconvenience. He set out west, following Nester's directions. His mind sifted through long-buried memories as his feet took him farther away from civilization.

Her reappearance, combined with Hux's, thrust him into a bloodier, more chaotic time. Which was saying something, considering the last couple of years. He'd been younger and stupider, but neither justification was sufficient excuse. Hells, they were the reason he had set out west in the first place, seeking something resembling peace.

Until tonight, he thought he'd put the gang behind him. Not just physically, but completely. He hadn't thought of them for years.

The storm of emotions currently raging in his chest gave lie to that belief. All he'd done was bury them in shallow graves, and they'd found it all too easy to crawl out.

The sun was rising when he felt the cadence of her breathing change. Though she made no other sound, he knew she was awake. He stopped and put her down on her feet. Then he stepped back and forced himself to meet the eyes of the first woman he'd ever loved.

"It's been a while, Narkissa."

10

Her first words weren't quite what he expected.

"Why didn't you kill me?"

The question landed like an accusation, like Tomas had committed a grave offense by not sending her to the gates. His first instinct was to raise his hands to calm her.

But that was the reaction of a younger man he'd worked hard to leave behind. Instead, he shrugged. "Don't blame me. Arrow missed your heart, is all."

She glared at him. "You stabbed me to keep me unconscious. I'm sure if you were so inclined, you could have made the wound fatal."

"I have questions."

She spat on the ground. "We were out east, working our way south down the Tershall. Had one particularly persistent marshal after us. Then this stranger appears as though out of nowhere. Not only does he know everything about Hux and the way he works, he knows all about us, and all about you. He offered us a princely sum to catch you alive."

"Why alive?"

"Don't know. He said that if he wanted to kill you, he could just do it himself."

"And you took him up on his offer?"

"We would have come after you for free if we knew where you were. The money was just a bonus."

Tomas frowned. Unlike Hux, he'd always been able to discern when Narkissa was lying. And she was holding something back. He pressed harder. "Hux never took a job he wasn't sure he could pull off. Y'all might hate me, but even with you and Hux being hosts, you had to know it was risky. Why take it?"

"Our employer wasn't the sort of gentleman who left us much choice."

"He bring an army unit?"

She shook her head. "Just himself, but it was enough."

Tomas raised an eyebrow. "That good?"

"Makes our fight last night look like stretching before a practice bout."

"Who does he report to?"

"Didn't say."

Tomas heard the implication in her answer. "But?"

"But he's definitely a churchman. The belief practically leaks from him. Not a very pleasant fellow."

"A host for the church?"

The last of her defenses broke under his questions. "Scariest man I've ever met, Tomas, and that's including you, back when you'd get angry."

Tomas digested the information. He didn't know what to make of it, exactly, but he knew it tasted sour. That the church wanted him dead was no surprise. That they had a host, skilled enough to frighten Narkissa, worried him. He knew he didn't have a complete map of the church, of the myriad roots it had extended throughout the country. But it kept revealing more of itself, and he didn't like what he saw.

Narkissa spit again. "So, I've told you all I know. Now, will you kill me?"

"I'd rather not."

"Then you've got one enormous problem, because the moment you give me a chance, I'm going to kill you. Now that it's only me, that reward will be enough to let me retire for the rest of my life."

Tomas grunted. "Thought you were supposed to bring me in alive."

"Dead still pays, and besides, now that I'm looking at your face, it's personal."

Tomas took a deep breath and let it out. What else had he been expecting? Soon he'd need to sleep, and he'd much prefer to do it without a wrathful ghost from his past chasing him.

He knew the answer, of course. He'd hoped that they would peacefully resolve their differences. Which, if he'd thought about it for more than a second, was a truly foolish idea. He'd have better luck convincing a wet piece of wood to catch on fire, using nothing but his stare.

Still, it was worth a try. "Don't suppose you'd be willing to just walk the other way?"

She looked at him as though he were speaking an unfamiliar language. Then she cocked her head to the side, like an owl, and he almost smiled. It had been a long time since anyone had given him that particular look, but she'd once looked at him that way often. "You left us for dead. You left *me* for dead. So, no, I'm not going to just 'walk the other way.' Are you daft?"

"I'm sorry," Tomas said. "Truly. You don't know how

many times I've gone back to that day and wished I could live it again."

She snarled. "Oh, I'm sure it must have been *sooo* hard for you, wandering free out here in the west while they hunted us through every city we hid in."

Her answer almost distracted Tomas from the point of the conversation. He was curious how the gang had escaped the predicament he'd left them in. Unfortunately, this morning wasn't the best time to ask. Whatever the answer was, Narkissa made him sure it hadn't been an enjoyable experience.

He tried again. "Is there anything short of killing you that would serve both our interests?"

Her answer came without a moment of hesitation. "You could fall on your own sword."

He looked up at the sky. "Right."

Of course she would put him in a tough position. She seemed more than willing to die, and he really didn't want to kill her if he could help it.

Wait.

Why hadn't he thought of that before?

It had been too many years since he'd seen her last.

Though she was prone to extremes, one fact about Narkissa had always been constant. She loved living. When they'd been together, it had been one of several recurring arguments about Elzeth.

Why had he allowed himself to become a host, knowing what it would cost him in the end?

She had understood that he was dying when he'd accepted Elzeth's unspoken deal, but she had never liked the tradeoff involved with becoming a host.

But here she was, a host herself, and practically begging him to kill her.

People changed. He was evidence of that himself. But this much?

Something else motivated her pleas.

A suspicion grew, a knot in the pit of his stomach, a guess that seemed all too likely to be correct. "Why do you so desperately want me to kill you?"

"To finish what you started," she said. "Did we mean nothing to you? Did I?"

Perhaps it was a truth, but it wasn't the full truth. He waited, knowing she would eventually tell him.

She looked left and right, as though making sure that nobody was around to hear her. When she spoke, he heard something in her voice that he'd never heard from her, not even when marshals were chasing them, threatening them with a life of forced labor.

He heard genuine fear.

"I'm dying, Tomas. I'm going mad."

11

Her answer only confirmed the suspicion he already held. Yet he still felt as though he'd just been run over by a train trying to make up time between stations.

He shouldn't. She'd been out of his life for years, and out of his thoughts for almost as long.

Some guilt lingered, stretching its tendrils through time to wrap around his heart today. But how long would he let the feeling steer his path? If he committed to righting all the wrongs of his past, he'd never move forward.

Had it been Hux standing in front of him, Tomas might have drawn his sword and cut the man down. Once there'd been respect between Tomas and the boss, but not anymore.

Narkissa, though, was different. Perhaps he'd been a fool, but once he'd believed they would be together for the rest of their lives. Leaving the gang hadn't been hard, but leaving her had ripped his heart into shreds. Pieces he never thought he'd sew back together until he'd met Angela.

"He said that he's got a cure. That the church developed

one. And that if we brought you in alive, he would give it to us," she said.

Tomas scoffed. "And you believed him?" Becoming a host granted extraordinary strength, but the cost prevented most people from grasping that power. Going mad and dying was inevitable.

Narkissa shrugged. "It would explain why a believer would pollute himself with a sagani. Even a slim chance is better than nothing."

He hadn't considered that. If anyone had a cure for the madness, it would be the church. No one conducted more experiments on hosts. Still, it seemed unlikely. "Do you know how it works?"

"He said it kills the sagani."

"Not for me, then," Elzeth said.

Tomas couldn't help but consider the trade. Elzeth had been a part of his life for so long, he struggled to imagine life without the sagani as a constant companion. But if it meant he could live the rest of his natural lifespan, perhaps it was a possibility worth considering.

Except he couldn't do that to Elzeth. Not after all they had been through.

Narkissa stepped toward him, and Tomas didn't back up. Once, her presence had intimidated him, but no more. "So, you see the problem. Either you kill me here, and put me out of my misery, or I pursue you all the way to the ocean, if that's what it takes."

Tomas' hand inched toward his sword. He didn't want to, but he also knew Narkissa well enough to believe every word.

"There is a third way," Elzeth said, "though both of you seem too wrapped up in the past to think about it."

"What?"

"Work together to steal the cure. If it exists, stealing it from the church opens up some tantalizing possibilities. Perhaps we could even separate host from sagani without one of them having to die."

"What's Elzeth saying?" Narkissa asked. She'd always been able to tell when the two of them were speaking, though Tomas was certain their private conversations didn't show on his face.

Tomas told her.

"If it means fighting Ghosthands, I'll pass, thanks."

"Ghosthands?"

"What I call him. He says that his sword technique is called the ghost hand, so it seemed like an appropriate name."

"Then we figure out how to get it without having to fight him."

She thought for a full minute, but he had the feeling he'd already won her over. "You know you like the idea. It's risky, foolish, and completely unexpected. It's the most fun you could have."

"Killing you would be pretty fun, too."

"I wish fewer people in the world believed that."

Narkissa cracked a smile. "You've changed, since then."

"I've tried."

"I like it. You always seemed like you feared something back then. There's not that much that frightens you now, is there?"

"I've seen some monsters I'd prefer not to again."

"Me, too." She was silent for a bit. "So, how's this going to work? You just going to trust me?"

"I'll take the manacles off if you give me your word you won't try to kill me."

She rolled her eyes. "Really?"

"Really."

"Fine, I promise I won't try to kill you."

Tomas produced the key from his pocket. "Turn around."

"Yes, sir." As he unlocked the manacles, she said, "You weren't so trusting back then, either."

He freed her wrists and gave her a gentle shove forward. "I'm still going to keep your weapons."

"Are you sure you found them all?"

"My search was pretty thorough."

She winked at him. "I bet it was."

This time, it was his turn to roll his eyes. He changed the subject. Talking with her brought up feelings he'd rather keep buried. "So, where to?"

"Don't know."

"If you caught me alive, what were you supposed to do?"

"That was something only Hux knew."

"Stop lying." He didn't believe her for a moment.

"Fine. There's a town north of here with a sizable church presence. We were supposed to take you there and wait for Ghosthands to meet us."

Tomas turned them north, and they began walking. "You know anything else about the town?"

"Hux did some research once he found out. The town is newer, like everything out here, but it has the potential to become a trading hub as more settlers move west. I hear one of the railroad companies is already laying track toward it. Probably helps that the church is very active in the area."

"How active?"

"We weren't sure. A mission and a rest, for sure. Hux suspected there was more going on, but couldn't find any information before we had to take off after you."

That made Tomas think of another question he hadn't had time to ask yet. "How did you find me, anyway?"

"Wasn't too hard, especially with Ghosthands helping. He told us you'd been in Razin, and he'd been roughly tracking your progress since then. He had reports from marshals and his own church people. Apparently, you're not very good at passing through places without a fight."

"They've been flooding every town with wanted posters. Hard for me to pass through unobserved. Leads to trouble."

"Sure," she said. "Anyway, we heard about your fight with the would-be bounty hunter, and knew the basic direction you were traveling. We spread out and checked every known farmstead. Didn't take us too long to find you."

Tomas cursed himself for his own laziness. He should have kept moving, but his desire for company had put Nester and his family in danger.

Hopefully, it was a lesson he wouldn't have to learn again.

After that, they settled into silence. Tomas thought about the past and the present, and he didn't dare guess what notions ran through Narkissa's head. Her mind had always been a mysterious place, and he suspected the years apart wouldn't make her any easier to understand.

About noon, Narkissa complained of hunger pains. Tomas pulled out food from the pack and they kept walking. The food lifted Narkissa's spirits, though, and soon she was regaling him with stories from their years apart.

None of the stories meant much to him. They were about people he barely knew in places he hadn't been for years. But he enjoyed the company, and, as she always did, Narkissa made him laugh. Every tale she told involved life-and-death stakes, and Tomas was certain she could make a trip to the outhouse sound like an epic war story.

In return, he told stories of some of his own adventures. Like her, he kept a safe distance from the tales that actually mattered. He didn't speak of Razin, or the mountains where he'd almost lost his life. Instead, he spoke of hunting failures, or the time he'd woken up to find himself being pursued by a surprisingly affectionate sagani.

With every story, it felt as if a piece of the wall between them was being torn down. He didn't know how long it would take to set things right, but every step, no matter how small, felt like it mattered.

By the time they rested for the evening, they had to have covered almost thirty miles. Tomas was tired, and although he once again split his food with her, he had the good sense to lie down on the opposite side of the fire. Within minutes, she was asleep and Tomas was staring up at the stars.

"Don't get too comfortable," Elzeth warned.

Tomas smiled. "You've never liked her that much. But I don't think you need to worry. I've never felt like I've really been able to trust her."

"She's got a way past your usual defenses, though. Don't think I haven't felt it."

"I know, and I appreciate the caution. I'll be wary. I suppose it goes without saying that I'm going to ask you to keep a close eye on her tonight? If she so much as stirs, I'd like to know about it."

"I will."

"Good. You know, the last time I fell asleep in the grass I woke up with a farmer debating whether to stab me with a pitchfork."

"I said I would!" Elzeth growled.

"Just had to point it out." Tomas smiled and watched the stars as they gently twinkled overhead.

Before long, he was fast asleep.

12

Not only did he wake up without a knife in his chest, he woke to the smells of breakfast cooking over the fire. He rubbed his eyes and stretched as he sat up. Narkissa squatted next to the flame, and for a moment, he wasn't sure if he was in a dream of the past or not.

"Don't look so surprised," she said.

Tomas grumbled something unintelligible that she ignored.

As they ate, his gaze kept wandering toward her. She noticed and guessed part of the reason. "I'm not so hard to figure out." She held out her hand. It trembled. "It's getting worse by the day. I want to live, and if I have to choose between trusting you and him, I choose you."

Tomas didn't ask the question that was on the tip of his tongue, but she did for him. "Yes, even after." She let out a long sigh. "Oh, I still want to kill you for leaving, but in my more forgiving moods, I know I would have done the same in your place."

Tomas figured that was as close to forgiveness as he would come.

"Don't read too much into it, though. I'd probably trust a grinning card shark in a gambling den more than I trust Ghosthands. He's not exactly one who inspires confidence in my twisted heart."

"He frightens you that much?"

"More than anyone I've ever met in my life."

Considering the company she'd kept over the years, that was making a statement. They finished their meal, and Tomas noted he felt more comfortable around her than he did yesterday. "I thought you were going to help me keep my guard up," he told Elzeth.

The sagani yawned. "I am. But her cooking is a lot better than yours."

Tomas chuckled. "Get some sleep."

Narkissa's eyes narrowed at his mirth. "What are you two talking about?"

"Elzeth likes your cooking more than mine."

She shook her head. "I've been a host for years, and I still don't understand you."

Tomas shouldered the pack, and they began their walk. "Why not?"

"I know that some other hosts name their sagani, but I don't think I've ever seen one with quite the relationship you and Elzeth have."

"Have you named yours?"

She scrunched up her face, as though the suggestion itself was offensive. "Never. We don't even talk."

"You don't?" Tomas couldn't hide his curiosity. He knew the experience of being a host differed from person to person, but he rarely came across anyone with whom he could speak freely about it. With the church prosecuting hosts whenever they could, those who shared their experiences hosting sagani made easy targets.

"No. I can feel it, and can feel its emotions, a little like how you described your relationship with Elzeth. But that's as far as it goes."

"You say you've talked with other hosts?"

"A fair number of them tend toward crime, what with the church restricting what jobs they can have out east."

"I didn't realize it had gotten so bad."

"You've been fortunate to be out here. Being a host isn't a crime yet, but I don't think it will be long until it is."

"But with all the hosts, none of them are like me?"

"No." She bit her lower lip. "It's more a sense than anything else. There are other hosts who name their sagani, and others who talk to them. It's not like there's anything you do that I haven't seen elsewhere, but it's the degree and the combination. You and Elzeth are unlike any other pair I've ever come across."

They walked through the day, making good time. Eventually, they came across a road and followed it. The roads were quiet this time of year. Most harvests had already been delivered, and the harvest festival was already past. Families prepared their houses for the long winter ahead.

When they neared budding towns, they left the road. It seemed likely the wanted posters would have spread this far, and Tomas wanted no more trouble than necessary. Narkissa offered to travel through the towns on his behalf, but he insisted she stay within sight. He feared that if he let her go into a town on her own, she might return with a mob.

They traveled that way for two days. Their pack became lighter, but Narkissa believed they were getting close, so they made no effort to replenish their supplies. Every day,

Tomas said his thanks to Nester and Bertha for their generosity.

They passed few people on the road, and one benefit of traveling with Narkissa was that she attracted most of the attention. She had a quick smile and shifted her weight often, drawing the eye. Tomas, in contrast, kept his head down and was quiet and still. It helped that the wanted posters implied Tomas wandered alone. Just by standing next to Narkissa, he became less suspicious.

He grew increasingly certain he could trust her, but the proper test would be when they reached their destination. It had occurred to him that all this was a ploy to deliver him to Ghosthands. That instead of searching for a cure, all he was doing was saving Narkissa the trouble of having to carry his body the dozens of miles to the town for her reward.

He didn't think so, though. The longer he spent with her, the more convinced he was she was telling the truth. All she wanted was to find a cure, and for the moment, she believed that working with him was the best path to obtaining it.

He didn't believe for a moment, though, that if the math in her head changed, if her route to survival meant betraying him, that she wouldn't do it in a moment.

As much as he hated to admit it, he liked that about being with her. It carried an edge of danger, an uncertainty that always kept him coming back, always trying to prove himself.

She'd always had that effect on him.

On the third day, they finally reached their destination, and as soon as it came into view, Tomas knew why Ghosthands had chosen this place in particular. Even from a distance, the magnificent spire of the church mission was visible. It towered over the rest of the town, and Tomas had no trouble at all imagining a giant, all-seeing eye at the top, judging the inhabitants below.

It was, he was certain, the largest church mission he'd ever seen on the frontier. And they were walking straight to it.

13

The sight of the tower chilled him to the bone. Tomas searched his memories, thinking of the enormous cities out east, seeking some structure he could compare it to. He failed. The tower had to be at least seventy feet tall, if not more.

"How does that thing even stand?" he asked.

Narkissa grunted. "You really have been out west too long. There are even taller ones in the cities now."

"Taller than that?"

"Substantially."

Tomas shook his head. "It seems like a powerful gust of wind would bring it down."

"I wish. As far as I know, they're as sturdy as thick stone walls."

Tomas swore under his breath.

"As much as I hate the church," Narkissa said, "only a fool would deny what they've accomplished since the war. They study everything from buildings to bodies, and they keep pushing forward. They experiment relentlessly."

"You almost sound like you respect them."

"In a way. I admire their determination to reveal the ways of the world. But they ignore any human cost. For all they've given us, they've also killed more people than any army, and they don't even blink."

"So, if anyone has a cure, it's them."

"Exactly."

They admired the tower for another minute, then Tomas turned to their more pressing problems. "You ever been here before?"

"Never."

"So, no idea what we're stepping into?"

"None at all."

"Perfect." Tomas studied the layout of the town. "I expected the place to be smaller."

"Same. I knew it was growing, but nothing like this."

"You never mentioned its name."

"Chesterton. I can go in and explore it for both of us, if you want." There was a challenge to her smile.

Tomas actually considered it, which probably said more about his newfound worry about the tower and what it represented than his trust in her. He shook his head. "You've brought me this far. Not much point trying to run now." He led them toward the town.

Despite the tower, Chesterton seemed much the same as any other frontier settlement. Perhaps a dozen people roamed the streets, and although the place was quieter and cleaner than Tomas expected from a remote town, he saw nothing else that made him want to turn tail and run.

The constant shadow of the tower, though, was like an itch he couldn't scratch. He could see it from anywhere in town, and he felt as though he were constantly being watched.

Despite his misgivings, he didn't see any wanted posters displaying his likeness. He breathed a sigh of relief at that. He hadn't realized how much he prized anonymity until he'd had it stripped away.

One of the first shops they passed proclaimed itself as a general store, and Tomas nudged Narkissa toward it. There were a few supplies he wanted, and a store seemed as good a place as any to learn more about the town. At the very least, it was close to the outskirts, so if they needed to flee, they wouldn't have as far to run.

When they stepped inside, Tomas saw they were the only customers in the store. From the way the woman behind the counter jumped when they entered, Tomas had the feeling they were the first customers in quite a while.

"Sorry to startle you," Tomas said.

The woman straightened her hair. It was a vivid red, which fell in curls around her face. As soon as she brushed it from her face, it returned. "No, I'm sorry. I was just daydreaming." She took her first good look at the two of them. Her eyes lingered on their swords, and her eyes narrowed at the sight. "What brings you two through town? Looking to become knights?"

That seemed an odd question, but Tomas ignored it for the moment. Somehow, he had the feeling anything close to the truth wouldn't sit well, so he told the first story that came to mind. "We're partners, exploring the frontier, trying to find a place to settle down. We were thinking we would stay here for a few days, then continue on."

The shopkeeper visibly relaxed. "Well, we're glad to have you here. I'm Leala, and this is my place, at least for a while longer."

Tomas and Narkissa introduced themselves. Narkissa

hadn't missed Leala's statement, either. "Are you planning on selling the store?"

"Looks that way. To tell the truth, you two are the first customers I've had in almost a week."

"In a town this big?" Tomas asked.

Leala thrust her thumb behind her, pointing toward the center of town. "Another general store moved in about six months ago. They're charging much lower prices than I can afford." Leala studied the two of them. Then she sighed. "And, I suppose I should tell you, the church strongly encourages everyone to purchase their goods from that store. It's run by a faithful church member. So if you two are believers, most citizens will look down on you if you buy here. Figured I should let you know."

"They're driving you out?" Narkissa asked.

"Seems that way. I was one of the first to settle here several years ago. But then the church came in with their mission, and the priest came by and asked if I would attend their services. When I gave him a polite 'no,' he was all smiles. He said I'd always be welcome, then left without another word. Three months later, a new general store appears, and though I don't have proof, I'm sure the church is giving them gold to keep their prices lower than mine."

Narkissa swore.

"I take it you two aren't believers?" Leala asked.

"We're not," Tomas confirmed. "Not much love lost for the church here, honestly."

"Well, if that's the case, I'm not sure how warm a welcome you're going to find here. We've had a lot of new settlers in the past year, and while it warms my heart to see the town growing, it's almost all believers. It's not as welcoming a place as it used to be, and no small number of my friends have already sold their property and moved on."

"What keeps you here?" Narkissa asked.

"Stubbornness," Leala answered. "I'm not so much opposed to leaving the store behind. Church certainly pays well for the land. But I came out here to be free, and it really rubs me the wrong way to have folks telling me what I can and can't do in a town I helped build with my own two hands."

"When you first saw our swords," Tomas asked, "you thought we might be here to become knights. Why?"

"It's what most people with swords are here to do." This time, Leala pointed north. "There's a fort up there where prospective soldiers train to become knights. I hear it's an intense place, but I've never been that close. Sorry to presume about your intentions, but if someone isn't a believer, about the only other people that come through are veterans looking for work."

"It's not a problem," Tomas said. "We've got a few things we need, and we'd be happy to purchase what you have. I don't suppose there's a place in town that might be a good place for us to stay for a few nights, is there?"

Leala grinned, and Tomas wasn't sure if it was because of his promise to spend money or because she had the perfect answer to his question. "There is a place, actually. Like me, I'm not sure how much longer he'll be in business, but he'll be excited to have you. Of that, I'm sure."

Tomas told Leala what they needed, and she helped him find what she had. Before long, they were well equipped, and Tomas had directions to a place in town they could stay.

Before they left, though, Leala gave them a warning. "Just so you know, even if you're not church supporters, it's best not to say so too loudly in these parts. The people here, well, they aren't casual believers. A lot of them live and breathe for the faith, and don't take kindly to any sort of talk against the church."

"Thanks for the warning," Tomas said. They stepped back outside, and even though they'd just met an ally, he couldn't help but feel like Chesterton was going to be a dangerous place for them to spend time in.

14

"What are you thinking?" Narkissa asked.

"That I really don't like the places you take me to."

"You could always leave. I'm not exactly forcing you to stay."

"How long would it be before you chased after me with several units of knights?"

Narkissa shrugged and smiled, but didn't actually answer the question.

"Seems to me that if there is a cure here, it's probably in the mission," Tomas said. "But I suspect two hosts visiting in the middle of the day is a piss-poor idea." He glanced at Narkissa. "Do locked buildings still fear your approach?"

"Of course."

That decided it, then. "Then I suggest we find the inn Leala spoke of. We can spend the rest of the day there, out of sight, then return to the streets after the sun goes down. With any luck, we can be out of this creepy town by the time it rises again."

Narkissa yawned and gave an exaggerated stretch. "And

here I was, hoping I'd be able to spend the night in a bed for once. You could join me, you know."

Tomas successfully managed not to roll his eyes. "Come on."

The directions Leala had given them were simple. Most of the shops and inns were on the main street, which made places easy to find. Tomas noted several businesses had the three wavy lines of the church painted somewhere on their facade, often near the door. They were usually small, but once he saw the first few, he couldn't help but see them everywhere.

Little badges of loyalty. Public proclamations of belief. He shook his head. Many of the stores that didn't have the mark looked abandoned, and Tomas didn't see any visitors going into or out of the unmarked stores that were open.

Leala had said little, but she'd pulled away the veil of ignorance from his eyes. Now that she had, there was something else that wasn't making much sense. He asked Narkissa. "Given what Leala said, why don't you think there are wanted posters up here?" He'd been keeping a wary eye, and so far he hadn't seen one.

The question brought Narkissa up short.

"Seems like one of the first places they'd show up," he said.

She considered the question. "Maybe. There are other explanations, too. Could be that Ghosthands didn't want any interference when we arrived here with you in tow. Could be they figured you would never be foolish enough to step foot here voluntarily."

They were both reasonable explanations, but neither unknotted the twisting feeling in his stomach. But they were drawing looks standing in the middle of the street, so he pulled her forward. The faster he could get inside, the better he would feel.

He found the inn with little difficulty. Like the rest of the town, the front of the building looked as though it had just been cleaned a few minutes before Tomas arrived. When he stepped inside, he felt a strong sense that he'd been here before. A moment later, he realized why.

It was nearly identical to Franz's inn, where he'd stayed so long ago. There was a place for him to leave his footwear. He pulled off his boots and stretched his toes. Then he went over to the small washbasin. White cloths, which looked so clean Tomas swore they'd never been used, were crisply folded beside it. He washed his face and hands, taking the time to scrub the accumulated dirt from his skin.

Narkissa followed his example without complaint, which was yet another surprise. She didn't respect tradition the way Tomas did.

When they were cleaner, they entered the next room, where the innkeeper waited for them. His long gray hair was pulled back tight, and he'd trimmed his beard to a narrow point just below his chin. His clothes were as white as the washcloths in the previous room, and Tomas couldn't find a wrinkle in them. The innkeeper bowed as they entered.

Tomas returned the bow. "Leala told us this might be a good place for us to rent a room while we're in town," he said.

"I'm honored," the innkeeper said. "Do you know how long you'll be staying?"

"Hopefully no more than a night or two, but we'll see. Our plans might change."

The innkeeper wrote their information in a book. He introduced himself as Agis, then showed them to their room. "Will you be staying for supper?" he asked.

"Please," Tomas said. Agis excused himself with a bow, leaving Narkissa alone with Tomas. He looked around. The room was as clean as any he'd ever been in. He had little trouble imagining Agis attacking built-up dust as though it were an enemy besieging a fortress.

Narkissa sat on the bed, then flopped back and stretched out languorously. She patted the sheets next to her. "Only one bed," she said.

"I suppose you'll have to sleep on the floor," he replied.

She made a pouty face. "You'd think after a few days together, you'd trust me more."

"I didn't trust you even when we'd been together for months."

His comment was offhand, his wit running ahead of his sense. But it still surprised him when he caught the brief hurt look on her face. "Truly?" she asked.

Tomas ran his hand through his hair. He'd rather fight a knight than dig up the past, but there was never a knight around when you needed one. He thought back to their days together, of all the fighting and chaos they'd sown. "No, not truly. I believed you would have died for me, back then."

"I would have, I think. Which made your leaving hurt all the worse."

Tomas had nothing to say to that. He'd already apologized, and wouldn't again. Nor was it possible to feel more guilt than he already possessed. He walked to the window and looked out over the streets of Chesterton. "We should get some rest while we can."

Narkissa looked genuinely disappointed. "You're not much fun anymore, are you?"

He considered protesting, but figured it was a waste of breath. He took off his sword and sat down against the wall.

"You could share the bed," she said. "There's plenty of room."

The offer was more tempting than he cared to admit. Every day with her reminded him of what he'd once had. What it seemed like he could have again, if he wished.

But he couldn't bring himself to trust her. She had plenty of reasons for wanting him dead, and he wouldn't make it any easier for her. "Get some rest," he said, and then, following his own advice, he closed his eyes.

15

B y the time Tolkin rose over the horizon, casting the darkened world in pale shades of red, their stomachs were full and their plans made. Agis' cooking was better than Tomas could have hoped, and the innkeeper seemed delighted to feed them until their bellies threatened to explode from the sheer volume of food.

Unlike Franz, who had quickly approached and befriended Tomas, Agis preferred to work out of sight. Tomas knew the man was busy. When he went to get his boots from the entryway after supper, he found them already cleaned. The washbasin had been emptied and refilled with clear water, and the dirty cloths ferried away to whatever magical cleaning process left them so white.

Tomas opened the window in their room and let his gaze wander over the streets and rooftops. Chesterton was so silent it almost seemed abandoned. When Tomas examined his memories from earlier that day, he realized he hadn't seen one saloon or gambling house. No wonder the place was so quiet. It was as boring as Narkissa thought he was.

"Doesn't look like there's anyone out," Tomas said. "Want to change the plan?"

Narkissa shook her head. "I'd rather be cautious."

"And you say I'm no fun."

She came over and stood beside him. Part of him wanted to step away, a cautionary habit. For the first time since they'd fought outside Nester's, she now had all her tools and weapons back in her possession.

Elzeth had argued that they should leave her unarmed. His argument, distilled to its essence, was "she tried to kill us, and probably will again."

It was a good point, but if the cure was inside the mission, it stood to reason the mysterious Ghosthands was there, too.

At least, that was the defense Tomas put forth. Elzeth hadn't bought it, though. "You trust her, don't you?"

Tomas confessed he did. Though he'd made a show of keeping his distance, he didn't expect her to harm him. Now that he looked back on the last few days, he'd trusted her ever since she confessed her madness.

After Narkissa made her own study of the scene outside their window, she turned to him. "Ready?"

He nodded.

"Kiss for good luck?"

He shook his head.

"You really are a bore." Then, quick as a cat, she was crouched on the windowsill. She reached up and pulled herself straight up the wall of the inn, her feet vanishing silently.

Though he'd seen her break into dozens of buildings, the sight of her in her element never failed to instill a sense of awe. Back then, they'd called her their wraith. No wall, no defense, no guard could stop her from going wherever she wished. Like a ghost, she simply appeared wherever she wanted to be.

Tonight, she climbed to the top of Agis' inn. From there, she crossed rooftops until she was standing at the intersection of the main street and the smaller side street that led to the inn. If not for Elzeth's aid, Tomas wouldn't have heard a single footstep.

He watched her as she crouched at the corner of the building. Then she gestured for him to follow.

He didn't have her agility, so he settled for dropping out the window and landing quietly in the street. He hurried forward, keeping her in sight.

As they'd planned, she scouted ahead. She made sure he could walk the streets unobserved, though it wasn't much of a challenge. They didn't see a single soul.

Tomas appreciated a peaceful town as much as anyone. But this? Chesterton sent a chill down his spine. He didn't even see any candles in the windows. It was as if the sun had set and every citizen had immediately gone to bed and fallen asleep.

Thanks to the lack of activity, they made good time across the town. Tomas kept an eye on the tall tower, but there was as little movement there as everywhere else.

Before long, they were in a shadowed alcove close to the mission. The tower, made of stone that had to have been carted in from a great distance away, marked the entrance to the mission. Behind the tower, the mission was a single long structure with a steeply sloped roof.

Narkissa pointed to the windows. "Barred."

Tomas grunted. "They really don't want their parishioners escaping once the service begins."

That brought a smile to Narkissa's face. "Or they want to keep people out."

"Odd, considering a mission is supposed to welcome people into the faith."

"Almost like they have something valuable inside."

He heard the hope in her voice, and it gave him pause. They hadn't talked about her descent into madness since she'd first made her confession. Most of the time, it was easy to pretend it wasn't real. Once or twice a day he would see a tremor pass through her entire body, but otherwise she was the same Narkissa he'd known then.

But this was important to her, and it wasn't hard for him to sympathize. Someday, perhaps soon, he'd be in the same situation. How far would he go if there was an actual possibility of a cure?

"Do you think the front door is unlocked?" he asked.

"Wouldn't want to use it even if it was," she answered. "If there's a way in, it's through the tower."

Tomas looked up. They'd discussed the tower back in their room. But now that he was looking up at it, he shook his head. "There has to be a better way."

Narkissa crossed her arms. "I'll wait while you find it."

She had a point. Missions never had back entrances. The church taught that the only way to enter a mission was through the front door. There was a whole ritual Tomas had never bothered to learn. They displayed their belief, even in their architecture.

But he really didn't want to climb that monstrosity.

She patted his cheek. "Don't worry. I'll hold your hand if you get scared."

Before he could argue, she ran across the street. She scampered up the side of the wall, between two windows, and grabbed the roof. A moment later, she was crouching on the roof, motioning for him to hurry.

He did, and although he believed he had acquitted himself well, her expression told a different story.

They crawled up the roof until they were walking along its apex. When they reached the tower, it looked like it had grown since Tomas had studied it from across the street. The stonework was better than he'd hoped, too. He ran his hands along the stone, finding nothing but the tiniest of handholds.

He'd suspected as much before, but now he was convinced. He had no chance of climbing this.

She held out her hand. "Give me the rope."

He handed over the rope, purchased from Leala, that had been coiled over his shoulder since they'd left the inn. She tossed it over her shoulder. "See you soon."

Once again, he was left with a protest dying on his lips as she left him behind.

Her skill was even more impressive now that he'd felt the wall for himself. She climbed the tower with an ease that made it look like she was climbing a ladder.

Her movements were smooth and controlled. She stuck to the wall as if someone had nailed her to it, and if she had any doubts at all, Tomas couldn't have guessed from where he stood and watched.

He thought then of her tremors, and of the madness that was slowly consuming her body and mind. He swore under his breath. If one struck her now, there wasn't a thing she could do about it.

He suspected the thought had already occurred to her, and that it didn't matter one bit. This had always been the way she lived. She risked everything, all the time, because it was the only time she felt like she was alive.

Forty feet in the air, clinging to nearly impossible holds,

hoping to steal a miracle cure, Tomas guessed she felt more alive now than she had in a long time.

His fears proved unfounded. She reached the top of the tower and slipped out of his sight. A few moments later, the rope dropped, reaching almost all the way to his head.

Tomas brushed his hands off on his pants and took a few steps back. With a brief running start, he propelled himself up the wall and grabbed the rope.

Although his ascent was far less challenging than hers, fear still gripped him as he climbed the tower. He worried less about losing his hold and falling and more about Narkissa cutting the rope as he neared the top of the tower.

As he climbed, the wind picked up, cutting through his clothes and sending a sudden chill from his hands up his arms.

A minute later he was safely over the ledge, crouching next to Narkissa. An enormous bell hung ominously behind them, a thin rope traveling through a small hole to the mission below. While he caught his breath, he looked around Chesterton.

Under other circumstances, he might find the town appealing. The streets were clean and the houses well-maintained. Though he found the nighttime silence unsettling, he didn't mind the quiet.

The only downside, and it was a big one, was that most of the town would want to kill him once they found out what he was.

Narkissa nudged him. "You going to spend all night staring into the distance, or are we going to break in?"

He turned and saw her pointing toward a trapdoor set flush in the stone floor. "After you."

She crawled over to the trapdoor and got her tools, so recently returned. Tomas, on a whim, reached out and pulled on the trapdoor. It opened without so much as a squeaky hinge.

Narkissa looked as though someone had taken away her entertainment for the evening.

Tomas rolled his eyes. "I'm sure there will be something in there you can practice on."

"Good." Narkissa put her tools away and disappeared down the trapdoor like water down a drain.

Tomas looked around once more, but the town was as quiet as ever.

He followed her in, hoping to find a cure that would save her life.

16

The inside of the tower, like the town outside, was bathed in Tolkin's pale red light. A narrow window, which reminded Tomas of an arrow slit covered with glass, was built into the stone about five feet below the trapdoor. The helpful moon gave them just enough light to see by.

Narkissa slithered down the ladder like a snake. Ten feet below the trapdoor opening was another floor. She tested the wood with her foot, and when it made no sound, put her full weight down. Tomas reached the bottom of the ladder soon after.

She gestured to the slit. "Decorative, or do you think the builders envisioned a day when an archer would have to defend this place?" Her voice barely carried to his sagani-aided ears.

"Knowing the church, probably both," he said.

Beyond the slit, there was nothing for them to see. The space in the tower was completely barren, the only detail of interest the rope which ran down the center of the room.

Tomas decided he had no desire to be in here when the bell above was ringing.

Another trapdoor was set in the floor, and this time Narkissa tested it before pulling out her tools. Once again, it opened silently. She shook her head, but kept her comments to herself. Through the crack, Tomas caught his first glance of the interior of the mission.

From his angle, all he saw were rows of pews. Enough that Tomas was certain they would fit the whole town inside, with a good portion of an army to spare.

Narkissa pressed her face to the crack, and for what felt like an eternity, she watched. Tomas settled down and waited. The wind moaned softly on the other side of the stone, disappointed it couldn't enter their little space.

Narkissa backed up and slowly closed the trapdoor. "There's someone inside, patrolling."

Tomas scrunched up his face. "What?"

"I never saw them, but I heard them. I think they're staying closer to the altar. Their route never took them under the trapdoor."

That complicated matters. "Can you get past them?"

"I might. Not sure your climbing is strong enough."

"Only one way to find out."

She shrugged, then opened the trapdoor once again. She slipped through the hole, and Tomas needed a moment to understand what she intended. Somehow, she'd found holds on the ceiling and was climbing across it. He poked his head through the hole, then shook it vigorously. He saw what she was grabbing, and she'd been right earlier. There was no chance he could follow her. Even with Elzeth, he'd slip and fall before he made it a dozen feet.

He pushed himself back up and thought. There was no ladder to ground level. He suspected the priest only put it up when they needed to perform some maintenance on the bell or tower. But they had rope. He tied one end to the ladder, which was secured both to the floor and ceiling of the space. He looped it around until just a few feet extended below the hole.

Then he let himself slide down the rope until his feet were near the bottom. It left him dangling high above the entrance, but it gave him a look at the whole inside of the mission.

First, he checked on Narkissa, but she needed no supervision. She climbed along the ceiling like a spider, her dark clothing blending almost perfectly with the deep shadows. His second look was toward the guard. He grunted softly when he caught sight of the patrol.

It was a single man, and young. But he wore the uniform of a church knight, and Tomas swore he saw the belief burning in the young man's eyes. As Narkissa had guessed, he was patrolling, but only seemed concerned with the altar near the back of the mission. He never once glanced up, nor did he pay much attention to the front of the building. Though Tomas dangled in midair, the knight's eyes never roamed anywhere near his location.

The scene set Tomas on edge. Why were the windows of the mission barred? Why was there a single knight patrolling only a part of the building? Nothing made sense.

His hands started to burn against the rope. The drop was too far for him to fall, so his options were following Narkissa on her impossible route or climbing back to the room above. He took one more look at the scene and ascended.

Back in the room, he shook out his hands.

They couldn't explore the mission without first subduing the knight. No doubt, Narkissa crawled toward him now with exactly that intent.

If Tomas wanted to take part in any of this evening's festivities, he needed to get down to the ground.

He went over to the ladder and uncoiled the rope from around its legs. Then he slowly lowered it down through the trapdoor. It didn't reach all the way to the floor, but the remaining drop was only about ten feet. Tomas could climb down, and the rope might serve as a route to escape the mission should they need it.

The knight didn't even notice the rope, which also struck Tomas as odd. Underestimating a knight was usually a quick route to a premature death. Tomas was wondering what he'd have to do to get this one's attention.

Once again, he climbed down the rope.

As more of the mission came into view, Tomas saw the knight had stopped his patrol and was now kneeling at the altar. He looked to be deep in prayer.

A shadow moved on the ceiling. Narkissa was almost directly over the knight.

Tomas let himself down the rest of the rope. When he was holding on to the last bit, he dropped. He landed without a sound.

He was about to take cover behind a pew when a door behind the altar opened. Typically, the door led to a room where priests stored the materials needed for the various sacraments the church offered. Sometimes there was also a small office for the priest.

This door, however, vomited five knights.

Knights who had as much in common with the young man at the altar as Tomas had with a tree. Each moved with the grace of a seasoned warrior, and Tomas quickly lost track of all the scars among them. The knight commander was a graying warrior who looked like he ate gravel for breakfast. When he spoke, his voice was scratchy, as though his daily breakfast had torn up his throat. "He told us you would come. Where is the other demon?"

The corner of Tomas' mouth turned up in a smile. They were about to find out, in one of the most surprising ways possible. He drew his sword, and the five knights mirrored the action. The young man at the altar looked to the commander, who nodded. The knight drew his own sword and joined the others. His stance was solid, but Tomas saw the point of his sword shake.

Tomas prepared himself for Narkissa's inevitable drop into the crowd.

But he wasn't prepared at all for what happened next.

A sudden spasm wracked Narkissa's body. She grunted loudly enough that it drew every eye up to the ceiling. The shadow slipped, then grabbed hold of the ceiling again. But even a spider's grip could fail.

She dropped, and there was nothing controlled about the fall. Narkissa plummeted, limp, to the stone floor below.

17

E lzeth flared to life, burning with a ferocity that singed the edges of the boundary between host and sagani. Tomas was in motion before Narkissa struck the floor, his footsteps echoing in the cavernous space.

Fortunately, the surprise of a body falling from the ceiling distracted all six knights for the precious seconds Tomas needed to cover the length of the mission. He reached the knights just as Narkissa hit the floor. Her body thumped against the stone, the crack of bones audible over his pounding footsteps. She bounced once and settled at an unnatural angle.

Not only would she be no help, he'd have to keep her safe from the knights.

Then Tomas was among them, his sword swiping their predatory blades away from her unconscious figure. He cut at the commander first, but the gray-haired man drifted away from the attack with ease.

Two knights swung at him from his left, forcing him right, where two others waited eagerly for him.

If he played into their strategies, not even unity would save him. There was still a limit to his speed, and five veteran knights working together should overcome his advantage.

So as he shifted right, he went low, sweeping his leg at one knight's knees. She might have dodged, but she'd already committed to her own attack. He felt her knee buckle inward as her partner's sword passed overhead. She fell, groaning in pain.

Tomas pressed against the lone knight. Their swords flickered in the pale moonlight. They passed one another and the knight fell, clutching the deep cut through the side of his neck.

The other knights maintained their composure, which disappointed Tomas. If he could kill even one more, he would breathe easier. Instead, the pair which had initially cut at Tomas advanced on Narkissa.

Tomas doubled back, inserting himself between them and her. He growled at them, and he thought they might have spooked, but the commander joined them and steeled their resolve. Tomas took a step back as the knight commander led the attack.

The seasoned veteran had years of experience and showed no hesitation in bringing his sword against Tomas. He wasted no motion, his cuts powerful and controlled.

Tomas had no choice but to retreat against the assault. Fighting the commander was like fighting a pair of average knights, and he already had a pair of knights to contend with. As he retreated, he saw the woman he'd knocked to the ground fight to regain her feet. If he didn't change the course of this battle soon, he'd be nothing more than a bloody mess on the mission floor.

But he saw no path to victory.

The only card he had left to play was unity. It risked plummeting him into the same madness that nibbled deeper into Narkissa's mind and body, but it was the only hope he had.

Then the novice knight saved him.

It wasn't the knight's intent. In fact, the knight had definitely wanted to take off Tomas' head with one powerful cut. He waited for an opening, and when he thought he saw one, he made his attempt.

Fortunately, Tomas was a host, and heard the young man's sharp intake of breath as he stepped forward.

Tomas ducked.

The bloodthirsty sword passed over his head, and the novice, expecting some resistance from his swing, stumbled between Tomas and the three knights led by the knight commander.

The commander was quick enough to check his blade, but the knight in the middle wasn't. The novice knight's neck rudely interrupted a cut intended for Tomas' skull. Tomas stabbed out, piercing the surprised veteran knight through the stomach. It was an unclean death, but Tomas had greater concerns.

As novice and veteran fell together, Tomas turned his attention to the fatally wounded knight's partner. The deaths of her friends distracted her, and Tomas cut her down before she recovered.

That left only the commander and the first knight Tomas had knocked down. For the first time since Narkissa had fallen from the ceiling, Tomas thought he might just make it out of this mess alive.

Which was exactly the moment he saw the injured woman stumbling toward Narkissa. One of her legs was at an awkward angle, and she was using her sword as a cane, but she still advanced steadily toward Narkissa's prone body.

The commander saw the same, and he positioned himself between Tomas and the slowly unfolding murder. "You'll never escape this mission alive, demon."

Tomas didn't waste the time responding. He shifted left, and as the commander shifted in response, Tomas darted right. But the commander mirrored that movement with ease, his sword persistently keeping Tomas from aiding Narkissa.

"Your attention should be on me, demon," the commander said.

Tomas growled, tired of the title, but he forced himself to ignore the commander's taunts. The older knight couldn't attack yet, because it would give Tomas the opportunity to slip past him. He only needed to keep Tomas in place for another three or four seconds. Tomas couldn't kill the commander that fast, either.

So he turned and ran.

If he couldn't fight his way through, he would go around. He backed up, and the commander made a fatal mistake.

He followed.

No doubt, he suspected Tomas would be easier to contain if the pews on both sides of the aisle limited Tomas' mobility. But his instincts, this time, were wrong.

Tomas took to the pews. With the additional strength and balance Elzeth granted him, Tomas had no problem running first across the seats, then across the thick backs. He circled around the commander, picking up speed. He skipped two pews at a time.

The commander tried to cut Tomas off, but had to make his way around the pews.

Tomas leaped from the last pew and hit the ground at a

full sprint. The injured knight reacted, but between her shattered knee and Tomas' speed, she didn't have a chance. Tomas gave her a clean death.

He stepped between Narkissa and the commander. Keeping her safe shouldn't be much of a problem anymore. Beyond the commander, only the knight he'd stabbed in the stomach still lived, but he wasn't moving much.

"I would let you leave," Tomas said.

The admission surprised him. It had been the urge of a moment. The knight commander deserved the death that was coming. Tomas suspected at least a few hosts had met their end at the sharp point of the man's blade. But he found he was tired of the fighting. Narkissa was safe for now.

The commander chuckled bitterly. "Your confidence is misplaced. I still haven't shown you my full skill." He twirled his sword with a flourish and sheathed it. He took a sword-drawing stance. "Come, let's finish this."

Tomas sheathed his sword, taking his own sword-drawing stance. Despite their differences, there was something about the knight commander he respected. "Who is it? Who gave you your orders?" Tomas asked.

"A man whose skill surpasses all others. You are nothing but a sputtering candle before his flame."

It wasn't the most useful answer he'd ever heard. "How did he know we were going to be here?"

"Who knows? We've been waiting a few days, using our initiates to lure you in."

That explained the young knight, but little else. "Where is he?"

The commander laughed again. "If you survive tonight, that is one question you won't have to worry about. He'll find you."

The knight seemed set on not giving Tomas anything useful. "Fine, then. Were your orders to kill us both?"

"Of course. All demons must die." The briefest flicker of hesitation crossed over the commander's face, as if he didn't understand why the question was even asked.

Tomas settled deeper into his stance. Elzeth burned, the feeling like a warm fire deep in his core. He moved first, and the battle was over in one pass. Tomas raised his hand, feeling the blood dripping from a shallow cut on his cheek.

The knight hadn't been lying. He'd hidden some of his strength.

"Close," Elzeth said.

Tomas grunted and looked around. He went over to the knight he'd stabbed in the gut. "Don't suppose you have any useful information?"

The knight swore at him, and Tomas gave him a quick death. Then he cleaned and sheathed his sword. Narkissa didn't look like she was going to be moving soon, so he used the opportunity to explore the mission.

The door the knights had poured out of did lead to a series of rooms, including a storage closet and an office. Tomas ransacked both, but found nothing of interest. He found a small collection of gold in the priest's office, which he took. Hux's money hadn't lasted as long as Tomas would have liked.

Tomas poked the floors and walls, searching for any sign of secret passages or chambers, but found none.

As near as he could tell, this was nothing more than an average mission, albeit with bars over the windows.

He scratched at his chin. The night's activities had raised more questions than answers, but they were alive, and that was something. He returned to Narkissa, who was starting to groan. He was there when she opened her eyes, and she frowned when she saw him. "Tomas?"

Then her eyes went wide, as if she'd remembered everything that had happened. She twisted her head left and right and saw the bodies lying across the floor. When she turned back to him, she was confused again. "What did I miss this time?"

18

Tomas sat on the edge of the bed, sipping at a cup of tea provided by Agis. He looked back at her sleeping form and, despite the circumstances, grinned to himself. Last night, he'd collapsed into the bed next to her and fell asleep until sunrise. It wasn't the evening he was sure she'd imagined, but they had shared the bed. He'd been so tired he hadn't given a single thought to the consequences of their escapades.

Now, it was those consequences that consumed him.

His first worry was Agis. The old innkeeper had seen them return the night before. Narkissa had lapsed back into unconsciousness as Tomas had carried her to the inn, so returning to their room through the window hadn't been a possibility. The poor innkeeper had nearly jumped out of his socks in fright when he'd seen them covered in blood.

But Agis' sense of propriety held, and he asked no questions, though he'd looked like he might actually explode with curiosity.

Once they found the bodies, though, this town would erupt in chaos. Given the connections most citizens had with the church, it wouldn't take much time for a mob to form outside Agis' inn. The only way to keep him safe would be to get him out of town as quickly as possible.

But Tomas couldn't do that with Narkissa unconscious. He suspected her sagani kept her asleep intentionally, healing her as quickly as it could. Nothing he did seemed to influence the sagani's behavior, though. He'd tried talking to it, explaining the situation. He'd even tried having Elzeth yell at it.

Leala was another worry. She'd sold them the rope they'd used to break into the mission, and if the town was looking for an excuse to drive her out, Tomas and Narkissa had just served them one on a platter.

Tomas stood and went to the window. The sun was just breaking over the horizon, and it wouldn't be long until he needed to decide. Perhaps Agis could get them a cart and they could load Narkissa and all Agis' goods into it.

He didn't like that option much, either. They would be too easy to catch by a dedicated posse.

And, of course, there were still too many questions around this mysterious Ghosthands and the cure. The way everyone spoke about him, even Tomas feared meeting the man. Personally, he didn't think the cure was real. More likely, it was just something Ghosthands used to manipulate Hux and Narkissa.

He swore softly. It would be nice if Narkissa woke up. Not only would her sword soon be necessary, she'd probably have a useful opinion on what to do next.

Well, one thing at a time, he supposed. First, he needed to talk to Agis. He could hear the innkeeper below, fixing them breakfast. Before he could reach the door, though, Narkissa stirred to life.

He hurried over to her side. Her eyes were sharp and

aware, the woman he was used to. "It happened again, didn't it?"

Tomas nodded.

"I remember breaking into the mission and climbing along the ceiling. Then it gets blurry. Were there knights?"

"Five of them, waiting for us."

"I didn't betray you."

Tomas believed her. They'd been together since the fight outside Nester's, and the knight commander didn't strike him as the sort of man who lied. Ghosthands had set the trap intending to kill both of them. "I know."

"You killed them? Thought I saw bodies."

"I did."

"Either knights have gotten worse, or you've gotten better. You couldn't have taken five back then."

"Got lucky. The one watching the altar had been a recent inductee. He got in the way of the veterans."

Her look told him she didn't quite believe him. "Still." She looked out the window. "Surprised you're still in town."

"I'm not running away without you again."

She bit her lower lip and refused to meet his gaze. "Did you search for it?"

"I did. I'm sorry, but I didn't find anything."

She digested the news in silence. Then she sighed and nodded. "Thanks for your help, and thanks for saving me. I think—" She paused, and clutched the sheets in her fists. "I think you should run. You should get as far away from here as possible."

Tomas sat down next to her and took her hand. The calluses on her palm brushed against his own. Narkissa was one of the toughest people he'd ever known, and she never ran from a fight. He would be a fool to dismiss her offer without consideration.

"What do you think?" he asked Elzeth.

The sagani turned the question back on him. "What do you?"

"I'm thinking that in the interest of a long and healthy life, we should take Narkissa up on her offer. Assuming we can convince her not to do anything foolish."

"She's dying," Elzeth said.

"But I don't believe there's a cure. There's nothing we can do about her dying."

"We can prevent her from dying alone."

"You didn't even like her that much."

"I still don't."

Tomas caught a hint of something else in the sagani's tone. "What?" he asked.

"I don't believe there's actually a cure, but we need to know for sure."

"Why?" Tomas asked.

"It's not about her, or even us. It's about the sagani."

"What about them?"

"You remember what Narkissa said? You've been thinking of it as a cure, but what she actually said was that it kills the sagani inside the host."

Tomas frowned.

"What if the church isn't developing a cure for hosts, but a way of killing all sagani?"

How had he not seen that before? The church wouldn't care about curing hosts. It was faster and easier to kill them. It was the sagani they hated. The enormity of the possibility struck him full force. A world without sagani? Was that the church's ultimate goal? The blood drained from his face.

"What does Elzeth say?" Narkissa asked.

"He says we should help you."

"Really?" The answer raised one skeptical eyebrow. "I

figured of the two of you, Elzeth would be the one telling you to run. He doesn't even like me."

Tomas cracked a smile. "He doesn't. But he's worried that the cure your Ghosthands is talking about is part of a larger plan to kill all the sagani."

"You just figure that out?"

"Unfortunately, yes." Tomas paused. "But even if there isn't a cure, we don't think you should die alone."

She squeezed his hand. "Thank you."

It was as if the years apart had never happened. He'd never run like a coward when she'd needed him most.

Tomas felt it, and it frightened him almost as much as Ghosthands was starting to. He returned the gesture, then let go and slid off the bed. "I'm going to talk to Agis. He needs to know the danger he's in."

His sudden departure surprised her, and for a moment, he thought he saw the hurt in her eyes. But it was gone a second later. "Good idea. Are you thinking what I'm thinking?"

"That your next plan is going to be even worse than killing six knights inside a mission?"

"Without doubt," she said, breaking into a wide grin.

19

Tomas left Narkissa and his doubts behind as he sought out Agis. Whatever the future held for them, the innkeeper needed to flee this twisted town before it was too late.

The old man wasn't hard to find. He was banging around in the kitchen as though he had a personal rule to slam his cast iron pan down every time he touched it. Tomas stopped outside the entrance to the kitchen, amazed by what he saw. Agis spun and shifted from side to side, absorbed in cooking breakfast for his guests. He tossed his pan around, and it seemed a minor miracle all the food stayed within.

The scents coming out of the kitchen might have attracted an army of hungry travelers, but if those same travelers were to watch the preparation, they might flee from the sheer violence of the process. It brought a smile to Tomas' lips.

Before he could clear his throat, Agis tossed the pan onto an open flame and turned around. "Breakfast will be ready soon. Is there anything I can help you with?"

Tomas' eyes narrowed. Given the cacophony emanating

from the kitchen, the old man must have been wary indeed to know his guest was behind him. Combined with the agility he displayed, Tomas began to think that there was more to the innkeeper than he'd originally guessed. "I was hoping to speak to you."

Agis gave one sharp nod. "I'll join you for breakfast, then, if you don't mind." He gestured toward the pan. "I'm making enough for three."

"It's rather more urgent—" Tomas stopped when Agis cut him off with a wave of his hand.

"It's about your adventures last night?"

"Yes."

"Then it can wait five minutes. Go get your partner and take a seat in the dining room. By the time you're there, I'll have breakfast ready."

"But you're in danger!"

"Not as much danger as you'll be in if your girlfriend finds out her breakfast is getting cold! Now, shoo!"

Tomas opened his mouth to object that Narkissa wasn't his girlfriend when Agis made a quick motion toward him. The next thing he knew, Tomas found himself in the hallway outside the kitchen, facing the stairs back to his room. His stomach rumbled, reminding him he hadn't eaten since the night before. He supposed he had spent the evening breaking into missions and killing knights, which would make anyone hungry.

He turned back to storm the kitchen again, then wrote it off as hopeless. It was still early. A few more minutes were unlikely to make much of a difference. They could eat quickly, warn Agis of the danger, and still get him out of town before most people were awake.

Tomas climbed the stairs and found Narkissa much the same as he'd left her. "What did he say?" she asked.

"He insisted on serving us breakfast, which will be ready in just a few minutes."

"You didn't warn him, did you?"

"I tried!"

Narkissa rolled her eyes. "Your judgment was always poor when food was involved. Did he offer you a fresh loaf of bread if you left him alone?"

Tomas didn't dignify that question with an answer.

Narkissa slid out of bed, and Tomas looked for any sign of the weakness she'd displayed the night before. But she moved as well as he'd ever seen. Better, even. He'd noticed on their journey to Chesterton, but she walked with a natural suppleness he didn't remember her possessing years ago.

He'd always found her attractive, and thanks to becoming a host, their years apart had been kind to her. That, combined with her dramatic increase in strength, made Tomas wonder about what might have been.

If only he'd had the courage to search for her earlier.

But he'd truly thought she'd died.

Now, though, the payment for the years of strength as a host was coming due. He feared that she had come back into his life just so he could watch her die again.

He followed her down the stairs, and they took a table. They were, of course, the only guests. Agis soon appeared with three plates of food. Tomas looked down at his meal and decided that staying for breakfast was the best choice he'd made recently. Agis had filled his plate from edge to edge with fresh bread, roasted meat, vegetables, and butter. As he stared at the food, every problem in his life slipped away.

Narkissa kept her wits about her, though. "Agis, we fear

that we've put you in danger. It would be best if you let us escort you out of Chesterton as soon as possible."

Agis' fork didn't even waver as he brought an enormous slice of roast meat to his lips. Once he finished chewing, he said, "You don't need to worry about me, although I appreciate the concern."

"I don't think you understand," Tomas said.

"That you two are hosts and killed some knights last night?"

Tomas almost coughed up his food. Thankfully, he swallowed it down. It would have been a shame to waste it.

Narkissa was halfway out of her seat. "How did you know?"

Agis waved Narkissa back to her chair. "You young people. So obsessed with possibilities you forget to see the world as it is." He took another bite of his food, and it seemed to Tomas the innkeeper was purposefully tormenting Narkissa with his behavior. "You two both move like master warriors, and if Leala sent you here, it's because you're no friend of the church.

"Then you come slinking back in the middle of the night, with blood on your clothes. I didn't figure you for mercenaries or criminals, so that ruled out killing any of the more innocent people in town. Which only left knights. And if you killed knights without getting too cut up yourselves, that would make you hosts. It's really the only story that makes sense."

Tomas scratched behind his ear and grunted. Elzeth laughed hard.

"So," Agis said, a grin on his face, "did I get it right?"

Elzeth was laughing so violently it made Tomas' stomach hurt. "Almost everything. She *is* a criminal, though."

Narkissa glared at him. "What?! You are, too."

"I was, once. I'm not anymore," Tomas protested.

"You're wanted by the church, the Family, and the marshals," Narkissa pointed out, her own grin smug.

Tomas would have flung food in her face, but it simply tasted too good. The truly unforgivable crime would be wasting it. "Fine. I suppose you have a point."

Then he turned his attention to Agis. "But if you figured all this out, then you must know how risky it is for you to remain here."

Agis shrugged. "You two are in danger, yes. But I'm not."

"How can you say that?" Narkissa said.

"My daughter is the priest for the mission."

"I'm sorry, what?" Tomas wondered, again, if he was slipping into madness. "I thought you didn't care for the church."

"I don't. If anything, I hate them."

Tomas held up his hand before Narkissa's head exploded. "Perhaps it would be best if you explained."

"I'd be delighted, though there isn't all that much to tell. I served for many years, back in the day. Was an officer in the war and acquitted myself well. They even offered me a promotion after. But I found no joy in fighting or commanding, and I had a family I'd spent too much time away from. I resigned and returned home.

"For a few years, things went well enough. My daughter, Edana, and I struggled to get along. For years, she'd gotten used to me only being present during winter, and even then, I was often involved in training new recruits. She grew used to the comfortable life my service provided, but I wasn't around much. I don't think she ever hated me. I was just— unnecessary—and she resented my sudden intrusion into her life."

Agis cleaned the last bites of food from his plate. "Then my wife took sick. The doctors did all they could for her, but she died within the year."

"I'm sorry," Tomas said.

"Thank you. It was obviously hard for us both, but much more so for Edana. She'd not encountered death before, and for her first experience to be someone who meant so much to her, it was even more difficult. She had many questions."

"So she turned to the church."

Agis nodded. "I'd always been ambivalent about them before. I even encouraged Edana to explore their beliefs. Mine, as a soldier, were less palatable. Now, I wish I'd been more honest with her. More willing to share the truth of the world with her. They embraced her with open arms, when it should have been me."

"To make a long story much shorter, she became a devout believer, and is now a priest. Being assigned out here was quite the honor, she tells me. The church has big plans for Chesterton, but she won't tell me what they are."

"You followed her out here," Narkissa said.

"She's all I have left. Though the church stole her from me, I came out here and started an inn. I've always liked to host guests, and I enjoy meeting the various travelers who pass through here. I don't know if Edana will ever forgive me for all the wrong I've done her, but I know that I'll be here on the day the church fails her."

"You don't think she'll attack the building?" Tomas asked.

"I suspect she'll come for you," Agis said. "But she won't move against me unless she's forced. So long as you two don't intend to barricade yourselves within here, there should be no trouble."

Narkissa looked like she was about to argue, but Tomas

cut her off with a glare. They couldn't tear Agis away from his daughter. "We'll leave now, then."

That was when Tomas noted that Narkissa wasn't paying attention to the conversation anymore. He turned his head to see what she stared at.

Out in the street, a woman approached the inn. She wore the white robes of a church priest, three wavy blue lines stitched onto each shoulder. Her resemblance to Agis was unmistakable.

Except Tomas considered Agis friendly and kind, and Edana looked to be neither.

Though he supposed he had made quite the mess of her mission.

She didn't approach the inn alone. Another five knights were behind her.

Narkissa's thoughts aligned closely with Tomas'. "What are they doing, breeding them here?"

Tomas stood from the table, immediately regretting how much food he'd eaten for breakfast. He looked down at Agis, who seemed to be content to watch the scene unfold. "I sure hope you're right about your daughter, sir."

The barest hint of a smile played upon his face, the only sign he was nervous about what was about to occur.

"Me too," he agreed.

20

———

E dana didn't hesitate on her way to the door. Tomas watched through the window, fascinated. At a glance, he didn't like what he saw. Her chin was so high in the air he was surprised she didn't trip as she walked. She radiated a smug sense of superiority, not unlike the look Agis had given them when he'd deduced last night's events.

She walked like she owned the town.

Although if anyone had such a claim, it was probably the priest for the local mission. Tomas watched her reach the door and wondered just how much Edana knew of what was happening here.

She didn't bother to take off her shoes in the entryway. She and her knights trampled dust and grime all over Agis' spotless floors as they entered the dining room, but the innkeeper didn't complain.

Edana took in the scene in a moment. Her eyes were sharp, the color of flint, and they reflected the intelligence of her father.

"Daughter, to what do I owe the pleasure?" Agis asked. His tone left no doubt he knew exactly why she was here.

She pointed at Tomas and Narkissa. "I'm here for them."

Again, Agis' attempt at appearing surprised was so blatantly false Tomas wondered what game the innkeeper was playing. "My guests? Why, they just arrived yesterday."

"And they killed six knights in my mission last night." Her next words were to Tomas. "Come with me now, before things get unpleasant."

"I'm afraid I'll have to decline," Tomas said.

Narkissa snorted in laughter. As the slowest eater, she was still finishing her breakfast, and seemed in no hurry to get the last bites to her lips.

Sparks flew from Edana's stare. "If you don't come willingly, we will make you."

Tomas sat down in his chair. It would slow his reactions if the knights attacked, but they had all stopped at the entrance to the dining room. He felt confident he had enough space to react. "So, let me get this straight. You come barging in here, threatening us, accusing me and my friend of killing six knights. But you've only got five behind you."

Edana almost spit out a hasty reply, but then Tomas' words struck home. Her eyes went wide as she realized her mistake.

It was the same one made by anyone who thought their authority was absolute. They got so used to having their way, they didn't even imagine situations where their opponents didn't capitulate.

"Now, let us finish our breakfast in peace," Tomas said as he tilted his chair onto its back two legs. "Your father is an excellent cook, and a captivating storyteller, besides."

Edana tried a different approach. "Agis, you are harboring criminals. You need to hand them over to us."

It was a desperate plea, and everyone recognized it. Tomas noticed Edana wouldn't even call Agis her father.

Agis turned to his guests. "If what she says is true, I'm afraid I can no longer offer you a place to stay. Please leave immediately." When neither Tomas nor Narkissa made any move to leave, he gave Edana a shrug. "I'll keep trying, but I'm afraid the villains aren't listening to me."

Tomas watched as Edana's weight shifted from one foot to the other. She was weighing the risks, wondering if her five knights could take the two warriors sitting down for breakfast. The problem was, she wasn't a fighter herself. She had no way of knowing.

So Tomas made the choice easier for her. He stood up, keeping his hands well away from his sword. He walked over to them, moving slow enough not to alarm anyone.

At least, he tried. The knights all grabbed their swords and prepared to draw. Tomas suspected only their confusion and a lack of explicit orders prevented them from all charging him at once. He stopped two steps short of Edana and not quite in front of her. "We're not looking for a fight."

"Then come with us."

"See, that will lead to a fight. It turns out I don't have much love for the church, and I really don't like knights." He paused and leaned forward dramatically, stage-whispering into Edana's ear. "Between you and me, I think they smell."

The knight commander of this squad stepped forward. She stopped beside Edana. "Give us the order, and he'll be in manacles a minute later," she said.

Back when Tomas had been in the unnamed units, he'd had a commander who had one rule they had all lived by.

Never do what they expect from you.

Tomas had found the advice useful throughout his life.

He summoned Elzeth and let the sagani burn bright

within. He leaned back, as though frightened of the knight and her threat. Her weight shifted forward, just slightly. Probably nothing more than an unconscious movement designed to intimidate him.

Tomas punched her in the stomach with his left hand.

He couldn't imagine the move succeeding in any other context. Had the knight expected it at all, she doubtless could have avoided it. But she'd been focused on his right hand, waiting for him to draw his sword. Combined with the sheer speed and power of a sagani-powered fist, she had no chance of reacting in time.

The commander bent like a sheet of paper being folded in half.

By the time she fell to the floor, Tomas had already returned to the position he'd started in. The knights drew their swords, and Tomas just held his hands up.

Edana's eyes grew even wider. Tomas suspected she'd barely seen the move. One moment, she'd felt like she was in control of the situation. The next, she was down her most talented knight. Unfortunately, Tomas couldn't find much sympathy for her in his heart.

Tomas met her gaze. "Not sure how good your math is, but now you have one less knight than when you came in." He glanced meaningfully down at the commander, who was gasping for air like a fish out of water. "Leave now, before someone gets hurt worse."

He could see the debate raging in her eyes. The sensible move would be to step away and live to fight another day. But she wasn't in a place ruled by logic and reason. She had entered the inn believing herself, at least on some level, the undisputed ruler of this town. Tomas' refusal to bend a knee stripped away some vital part of her identity.

Which would only make her angry.

Tomas was ready to draw. He hoped his statement was loud enough they wouldn't ignore it, but there was no telling with believers.

The only person in the room who moved was Narkissa, who finished the last of her food, belched loudly, and stood up and stretched. "We doing this, or what?"

Her confidence poked the last hole in Edana's facade. The priest sensed, rightly, that she didn't have a chance. Even the knights took a step back as Narkissa reached for her sword.

Edana jabbed a finger at Tomas. "We'll be back." Then she shot a glare at her father. "And I never thought you'd stoop so low."

Her last shots launched, she ordered the knights to retreat. They gathered up their commander, still searching for air, and escorted her out of the building. Once the door closed behind them, Tomas let himself relax.

"Your daughter is a real charmer," Narkissa observed.

Agis nodded. "Belief has twisted her personality. I remember her as a kind-hearted child, and I hope that underneath everything the church has made her, some part of that child still exists."

"Well, what do we do now?" Narkissa asked Tomas.

Tomas watched Edana as she gave orders to her knights to remain outside the inn. She would rush to get more soon. Which meant nothing good for either of them. Luck had been on their side so far, but they couldn't count on it for much longer. "If there's a cure, it's either in the church rest or at the fort Leala told us about."

"I could say the same of Ghosthands," Narkissa pointed out.

"You also get the feeling he's around?"

She gave one sharp nod.

Tomas aimed his next question at Agis. "If the church was hiding something valuable here, where would it be?"

His answer came immediately. "The fort."

"Can you give us directions?"

Agis nodded.

Elzeth butted in. "You remember the fort is filled with knights and knights in training, right?"

"I haven't forgotten."

"Ah, good. Well, this should be exciting, then."

21

Fortunately, Edana didn't have enough knights with her to form an appropriate perimeter. Either that, or it never occurred to her to order them to watch the back. Tomas gave Agis most of the gold he'd accumulated over the past couple of weeks as thanks for the hospitality. Then he grabbed Nester's pack and they left out the rear.

They escaped just as the citizens of Chesterton began to rise for the day. Fortunately, they were beyond the town's limits before their leaving had any chance of raising an alarm from alert neighbors.

Tomas was glad to be gone. He'd checked again with Agis, afraid the old man would suffer for sheltering them. Agis believed that Edana wouldn't do anything meaningful to him. Tomas had finally relented under the innkeeper's certainty.

The fort was only a few miles away by road, but Tomas and Narkissa took another route, given to them by Agis. They would circle wide away from the road and come at the fort from another direction. Agis believed it would keep them out of sight.

Tomas wasn't sure it mattered. If their assumption was correct, and Ghosthands was in or around Chesterton, he knew the two of them would eventually have to make for the fort. Especially if that was where the cure was being held.

"You sure know how to take ladies to the most welcoming places," Narkissa said, interrupting his thoughts.

"As I recall, the destination was your idea."

Something was on her mind. He saw it in the way she looked at him, the way she always looked like she was about to speak, but kept holding herself back. Eventually, she found the courage she'd been searching for. "It feels good, being back together like this."

He'd been thinking the same. Back in the inn, he'd never questioned that she would support him. Against five knights by himself, he wasn't sure what he would have done. He'd gotten lucky last night. But with Narkissa behind him, he'd felt no worry at all. It was the first time he'd felt that in a long time. He didn't worry about protecting her, or of her being in danger in a fight.

She had lifted a burden from him and made him feel lighter than he had in many years. "I agree." His memory traveled back to that night, so long ago, when he thought she had died.

They'd never expected the bank to be a trap. As far as Tomas knew, the thought had never even occurred to Hux. It was just another job. One that would hurt the other side and allow them to live like royalty for a few months. They spent as much time discussing how they'd spend their riches as they did planning the theft.

They had stationed him on the roof of the bank as a lookout, while Narkissa used her skills to let them through the front door as though they had the keys to the place. If any passing patrols paid the bank too much attention, Tomas was supposed to drop from the top and remind the local soldiers of the dangers of too much curiosity. The sounds of fighting would alert the others, who would come out and support Tomas if needed.

At least, that had been the plan.

Instead, dozens of marshals, supported by two squads of church knights, had emerged from their hiding places and besieged the bank like it was an enemy fortress. Tomas didn't even have time to warn the others, and there was no way he was jumping down into that mess.

He'd leaped from the roof of the bank to an adjoining roof, eventually putting enough space between himself and the bank that he could watch from safety.

He'd stood, silent in the shadows, as the people closest to him were hauled off, bloody from the fight inside the bank.

"What happened after they caught you?" he asked.

"I think, more than anything, they wanted you," Narkissa said. "It was the one reason I was sure you hadn't turned on us. All they wanted to know was where you were. We told them, of course. Let them know every nook and cranny you'd ever hidden in. But they never found you, I take it."

"Eventually, but not for a while."

She grunted, the news coming as a surprise. "Anyway, they put us to work on the railroads. Brutal work, supervised by even more brutal marshals. I made it about six months before I was sure I was going to die. Hux was the one who saved us. Put his big brain to the task and eventually figured out a way to break free. We've been on the run ever since."

Tomas fought the urge to apologize again. He'd heard plenty of stories of the horrors of the railroad gangs, but there was nothing he could do to take it back.

"The experience gave Hux an even sharper edge. He swore he'd never let himself get captured again. He was the one who decided we should become hosts."

"How'd you do it?"

"He heard of a place where sagani gathered. Had me try first. Went out there, and when one approached, I cut my wrists."

Even though Tomas had expected something along those lines, the confession still caused his step to falter. A host was only born on the brink of death. His own transformation had been accidental. But he could imagine Narkissa drawing a blade across her own wrists. She'd always been willing to risk her life for either fortune or excitement.

She pulled out a knife. It was one Tomas recognized, because he'd given it to her many years ago. "I used this one. Figured if I didn't become a host, I'd at least die making a point."

"I'm glad it worked."

"Me too." Her gaze traveled to the past. "Was it a magnificent experience for you, too?"

Tomas shook his head. "Not particularly."

"The sagani I saw was a bird, bigger than a crow. It looked like it was on fire, but when it landed on me, I felt no heat. Maybe it was just the blood loss, but it was the most beautiful creature I'd ever seen."

She spoke with a reverence that caught Tomas off guard. She was a woman who pissed on churches when she was drunk, mocking the very idea of something being sacred. Becoming a host had changed her in more ways than one.

"After that, Hux did the same. He couldn't bring himself to cut his own wrists, so I did it for him."

"Hard to imagine Hux being that trusting," Tomas said.

"Not when you knew him," Narkissa agreed. "But the work gang changed him. It gave him an edge, but it was almost too sharp. He was just as likely to hurt himself as someone else. It was hard, near the end, knowing what madness was sagani-induced and what he'd developed on his own. I think a part of him knew it, though, and knew he needed someone to keep him in check. After a while, I was the only one left."

"What did you do?"

"At first, we kept fighting the same war we'd been fighting when you were with us. We hit banks, believing we were crippling the government. But the pursuit grew with each new job. Hux kept us ahead of the authorities for a few years, but eventually we couldn't delude ourselves any more. We stopped going after big, juicy targets, and instead focused on staying alive. Eventually, the marshals and the church pushed us farther west. That was where Ghosthands found us, just a couple of weeks ago."

She stretched her neck, and Tomas heard several of her vertebrae crack. "What about you? What happened after you fled?"

"I fell in with another gang. They ended up betraying me, and I got captured by the church for a bit."

He could sense that she wanted to say, "serves you right," but she kept her lips sealed. "Got tortured for a few days, but made friends with an inquisitor and escaped. That was when I decided I'd had enough. I went west, looking for a new start, or at least, to get away from it all."

Then he told her the full version of what he'd been through.

When he finished, she reflected on his tale for a few moments, then said, "I think it sounds like you've had a better time."

"Don't forget the part where I got tortured."

"It was only for a few days. Stop being such a baby."

Tomas chuckled and shook his head. She was right. He had missed this, more than he thought possible.

Their mirth ended as they came to a rise in the land and heard horses and soldiers on the other side. They dropped to hands and knees as they reached the crest, crawling slowly until the fort came into view.

As far as forts went, it was far from the most intimidating one Tomas had ever seen. But that didn't mean it wasn't formidable. The wooden walls stood three times his height, and knights walked a patrol of the top. The fort was a perfect square, and at each corner, they had built a small square tower to protect guards from inclement weather.

Tomas counted more than a dozen knights at a glance, which led him to believe there were probably at least twenty in the fort total. The sounds they'd heard earlier came from a small group of knights racing their horses around the fort as the ones on the wall cheered them on.

"Chipper group, aren't they?" Narkissa said.

Tomas ignored her. He knew about the forts where knights trained, but for obvious reasons, had never gone near one. He found the sight fascinating. From his vantage point, he could see into the heart of the fort and he could watch the knights sparring with one another.

Their practice matches reminded him of his own upbringing in the sword school. Masters wandered between the duels, pointing out their observations. The only difference was these sword masters didn't carry around switches for punishing any perceived disobedience.

As one would expect, the knights were skilled. Tomas couldn't make out the details of their practice, but their wooden practice swords blurred together in intricate patterns. He swore. "I knew this was going to be hard, but I didn't think it was going to be this many knights."

"Think we could call them out one at a time and rely on their sense of honor?" Narkissa asked.

Tomas grunted. "The only honor they're going to be competing for is who can stab us the most times."

As he kept watching the fort, something tickled the back of his mind. Somehow, this fort was wrong, but he couldn't figure out why. He looked for some detail that was out of place, but the fort refused to give up its secret.

It wasn't until he'd given up and was looking around that he realized what was wrong. "Aren't you supposed to build forts on higher ground?"

Narkissa frowned. "You'd know better than me, but I would think so."

The only reason Tomas could look into the fort was because he was higher than the walls, which made no sense. He and Narkissa were on a rise and the fort was lower. In fact, it was in the center of a large, roughly circular depression, ringed by the very rise he was on top of. It was at the bottom of a wide, shallow crater.

"Why build there?" he wondered aloud.

"Easier to dig a well?" Narkissa ventured.

"Possibly, but I have a hard time believing they would choose such a vulnerable position just so they didn't have to dig as deep. The church wouldn't build there without a specific reason." He made a slight gesture at the surrounding land. "Literally anywhere within a mile would have been a better choice."

He resumed searching for that one telling detail, but he couldn't find it. He was just about ready to suggest they circle around the fort so they could observe it from the other side when Elzeth spoke up. The sagani had been strangely silent all day.

"I know why they built it there," he said, fear and resignation present in equal measure in his voice.

"Why?" Tomas asked.

"Because there's a nexus down there."

22

Tomas stared at the fort with fresh eyes. "You sure?" he asked Elzeth.

"I am. The longer we stay here, the more clearly I feel it. There's a nexus somewhere close."

Before he and Elzeth could continue their conversation, Narkissa interjected. "We should go down there."

Tomas frowned. "Now? Why?"

"Because..." Her voice trailed off. She cocked her head to the side in that owl-like manner of hers. "It's the right thing to do?" She frowned. "Why did I just say that?"

Elzeth's answer was acidic. "If she'd paid any attention to her sagani over the years, she'd know why."

Narkissa was shaking her head, muttering to herself. Tomas took pity on her, despite Elzeth's vindictive mood. "You're feeling your sagani's desire."

"Its desire?"

Some of Elzeth's bitterness crept into Tomas. "Didn't realize it had those?"

"No. I mean... what?" She looked as if she didn't even know where she was.

Tomas scooted closer to her, so that their shoulders were touching. She needed something to ground her, something to keep her in the present. He pointed toward the fort. "Somewhere down there, there's a nexus. It attracts your sagani. That's what you're feeling."

"A nexus?"

"I don't know what it is, either. A source of tremendous power, and it has some sort of connection to the sagani. The church wants them, badly, though I couldn't guess why."

Slowly, Narkissa seemed to return to herself. "So, I'm not going mad?" She caught herself. "At least, not more than usual?"

"No, you're not."

"Good." She looked down at the fort. "I don't know how we attack that and hope to stay alive. That's far too many knights, even for both of us."

"I know. Maybe there's a way we can draw the knights away."

Narkissa scoffed. "That, I'd love to see. If there's both a nexus and the cure, they won't leave even if we set the whole place on fire."

Tomas' mind churned over the problem. "They have to care about the town, though. Between last night and this morning, they already sent eleven knights that direction. It's possible we might draw some away if we cause enough chaos in Chesterton."

"That's an awful lot of chaos."

Tomas chuckled softly. "True, but have you met yourself? Hells, you probably wouldn't even need to try. I'll just give you the last of my gold and a jug of wine and it's pretty much a guaranteed thing, right?"

Narkissa grunted. "You're not wrong." Her good humor

faded. "I've missed this. Hux wasn't much fun after he became a host."

Tomas snorted. "I've always wondered where you get your idea of fun. Most people would piss their pants at talk of attacking that many knights."

That returned her good humor to her. "Eh, life is short and a miserable experience. Might as well make the most of it while we can. But if we are serious about doing this, I think there's something I need to tell you. I'm—I'm not sure how much you can rely on me."

Tomas almost laughed at the absurdity of her statement. "You want me to do this on my own?"

"No, it's just..." She took a deep breath. "The madness is worse whenever I use my sagani. So I don't know how much you should trust me to help you."

He shouldn't have been surprised, but he'd never thought of how the madness of the sagani might affect her. Of course, using the strength of the sagani exacerbated her challenges. But it made their task twice as difficult, and it had already been near impossible. "Don't suppose you want to just go down there and ask them nicely?"

"It might be our best plan. At least, it results in our deaths the quickest."

As they debated, they heard horses approaching. A few moments later, three horses crested the rise. They were on the road from Chesterton, and Tomas recognized the knight commander from their encounter earlier this morning. She looked like she'd swallowed something sour.

Narkissa's breath caught. "That's him," she said.

Tomas had wondered as much. The two riders on the wings of the formation were knights. There was no mistaking their uniforms. The man in the center was a different breed, though. He wore a sword, but his clothes were plain traveling clothes. Though Tomas couldn't point to any single detail to explain his feeling, just looking at the man unsettled him.

The riders were admitted through the front gate without slowing down. The guards recognized the man, and from the way they bowed to him, had no small amount of respect for him.

The sight of a knight bowing to a host left a bitter taste on Tomas' tongue. "You sure he's a host?"

"He has to be," Narkissa insisted. "There's no other way he could be as fast as he is."

Though he hated the thought, he wondered if this was another form of her developing madness. She predicted his thoughts with little difficulty. "And no, my madness hasn't altered my perceptions. He really is that good. If Hux were alive, he'd say the same."

Tomas didn't say what he was thinking, which was that using Hux as proof of honesty was about as sensible as using a sieve as an umbrella. Instead, he nodded. He believed Narkissa. The knight commander from the mission had also claimed that Ghosthands possessed extraordinary skill.

Tomas smirked as he wondered what Narkissa would think if she knew a knight commander was the best support of her claim.

The only way he would know with absolute certainty was to cross blades with the man. The longer they stayed around Chesterton, the more likely that seemed. "I'm guessing we don't want to attack the fort when Ghosthands is there?"

Narkissa's grunt was answer enough.

They settled in to wait. The presence of the knight

commander meant that Ghosthands already knew about the events of the morning. Tomas hoped Agis hadn't suffered repercussions for his decisions. He might have trusted his daughter not to harm him, but Tomas suspected Ghosthands was a different story.

The rest of the fort didn't seem too concerned by the new arrivals. The race around the perimeter of the fort had long since finished, and a new one was now in progress. Tomas guessed the races served both as an opportunity to let off a bit of steam and practice their riding. The knights on the training ground continued their sparring.

As much as he detested the church, he admired their efficiency, how nothing was limited to a single purpose. The fort here was a training ground for knights, but it also guarded a nexus. Perhaps it even housed a cure. It was a trait he'd observed from the church before. Why settle for one purpose when you can achieve many at once?

The thought made Tomas reconsider recent events. One simple question had troubled him ever since he'd learned about Ghosthands. If the swordsman was as terrifyingly good as everyone believed, why didn't he just attack Tomas straight on? He had no excuse not to.

Tomas could understand the hiring of Hux and the old gang. If the intent was to take him alive, there was no one better suited to the task. Hells, Hux had come close enough to succeeding. They'd also done the grunt work of tracking Tomas down.

But Ghosthands' actions in Chesterton made less sense. Why risk the knights? The church went to no small expense to make them the best warriors in the nation. They weren't mere pawns to be sacrificed on a whim.

There had to be another purpose to Ghosthands' actions. The more Tomas thought about it, the more worried he became. The hunter had predicted Tomas' moves well enough thus far. What did he have in store for Tomas next?

Observing the fort gave Tomas nothing but time to worry. As the sun rose and neared the midpoint, the knights who had been training disappeared into one stout building. Tomas suspected it was for lunch. A while later, they emerged and took their places on the wall while the others ate. The new contingent on the wall was joined by none other than Ghosthands himself. He walked the perimeter of the wall, his eyes roaming over the grass surrounding the fort.

Tomas and Narkissa remained still. They were in tall grass, and although they weren't well camouflaged, a guard would have had to stare straight at them for a while to spot them.

Ghosthands made two circuits of the wall, and the knights always offered him curt bows. Then he descended from the wall and disappeared.

"What do you think?" Tomas asked. "Should we keep watch, or try something else?"

"Such as?"

Tomas admitted he had no better ideas. They could go investigate the rest back in Chesterton, but he was increasingly certain the cure was here with Ghosthands and the knights.

So they waited.

Eventually, another pair of knights came to the fort from Chesterton, and Tomas again recognized them from the morning. They were only in the fort briefly before they left, taking with them the two knights who'd ridden in with Ghosthands.

Tomas had a sinking feeling in his stomach. Their plot was coming together, whatever it was.

Ghosthands confirmed Tomas' guess when he appeared at the gate of the fort a few minutes later. He stretched, then turned toward where Tomas and Narkissa hid in the grass.

Without hesitation, he walked directly toward them.

23

If Tomas had entertained any lingering doubts in his mind about Ghosthands' destination, they were quickly dispelled when the assassin waved in their direction.

Tomas grunted. "So, you think he knows we're here?"

Narkissa snorted. "No one could have seen us from the walls."

"And yet your friend is waving." Tomas moved to push himself to his feet, but Narkissa grabbed his shoulder and held him down. "He could be trying to get us to show ourselves."

"He's heading straight for us." Tomas removed her hand from his shoulder. "Either he's got the best vision of anyone I've ever met or he figured out where we were some other way. Regardless, he knows we're here."

There was no faking the fear in Narkissa's eyes. She was terrified, and that did more to convince Tomas of the danger than a hundred whispered warnings. This was, after all, a woman who didn't hesitate to suggest attacking a fort full of knights. Hells, he'd once seen her jump from a fifty-foot cliff to the water below, not even sure if the water was deep.

But they couldn't run, and they couldn't hide, so all that remained was to fight. He pushed himself to his feet. As much as he wanted to walk forward and show Ghosthands he wasn't afraid, he remained rooted in place. He didn't expect to find rifles on the walls, for the knights detested the weapons almost as much as he did. He didn't care to test his expectations, though.

Ghosthands stopped ten paces away, allowing Tomas to study him up close for the first time. At a glance, he didn't appear all that impressive. He looked to be a few years older than Tomas, but given the way hosts aged, that meant little to nothing. His features were otherwise unremarkable. He was of average height, and his loose clothes disguised his strength.

Still, there was something unsettling about the man. Though he stood no more than an inch taller than Tomas, Tomas felt as though he looked up at a giant. He didn't possess the wide-eyed appearance of so many fanatics Tomas had crossed paths with over the years. His eyes were dark and far colder than the nights up north. "Tomas, I presume?" He had a gravelly voice, as though he wasn't used to speaking.

"The one and only. And you are?"

"No one of note. Will you surrender peacefully?"

"Not really something I'm much into, if I'm being honest," Tomas said. "But why the games?"

"Games?" The man looked genuinely confused.

"I can see why you sent them," Tomas pointed toward Narkissa, who was slowly standing up, staying well behind him. "But why the knights? Why all this? To hear her tell the story, you could kill me with one hand while sipping tea."

Ghosthands smiled, and Tomas decided it was one of the most terrifying sights he'd ever seen. "Perhaps your friend is simply misremembering. I've heard that can happen to your kind."

Tomas' eyes narrowed. "Aren't you a host?"

"No." Tomas knew there was a punchline coming, but couldn't guess what it was.

Ghosthands didn't keep him waiting long. "You two are mere hosts, selling the temple of your body to the demons in exchange for a temporary and fleeting power. I am a master of the sagani within me."

"What?" Tomas blinked, trying to understand what Ghosthands meant.

The assassin gave him no time to decipher the cryptic answer. "Did you know the church has hundreds of pages of information on you, Tomas?"

Tomas felt as if he was stumbling backward, retreating from an onslaught of precisely aimed verbal cuts. He hadn't been sure what to expect of Ghosthands from Narkissa's description, but this certainly hadn't been it. "Must be thrilling reading."

"It is, actually. I copied it all by hand and brought the copy with me. You're an enigma, Tomas. A mystery. One whose solution might help us unravel all the remaining questions we have about this world."

"Maybe y'all should try treating me a bit more kindly, then."

Ghosthands proceeded as though Tomas hadn't spoken. "You are still, as near as we can determine, the longest-lived host we've ever come across. Most go mad within a handful of years. A few last longer. But your relationship with the demon within you is truly unique. Do you still talk to it?"

Elzeth interjected. "I'm getting a terrible feeling about this."

"You and me both." Tomas no longer wanted to continue this conversation with Ghosthands. He couldn't forget why he was here, and he tried to change the subject. "Do you have the cure?"

"Do you want it, too, Tomas? Do you want to rid yourself of the demon that's been living within you for years? Does the sin of carrying Elzeth wherever he wants to go wear on you?"

Elzeth flared to life inside of Tomas, despite Tomas' wishes. Tomas' hand twitched toward his sword. He froze it in place, but Ghosthands had noted the movement. "Even now, you fight against it. Some part of you, long buried, knows that I bring the answer. That you've finally found someone who can lift the burden from you."

Elzeth raged inside Tomas. He felt like a caged animal, barely contained by Tomas' ribs. Never had Tomas felt Elzeth respond so strongly to words alone.

"Do you have the cure?" Tomas repeated.

Ghosthands' left hand disappeared into a pocket and emerged carrying a small vial. It was filled with a clear liquid. Ghosthands shook it. "Is this what you're looking for?" He held it up to the light and pretended to examine it. "So many years of research went into this."

Tomas held out his hand. "Give it to me."

The vial disappeared back into the pocket.

Tomas almost attacked him. But Ghosthands no doubt expected it.

Ghosthands looked at the sun, as though judging the time. "If I were you, I'd be less concerned about the cure and more concerned about the friends you made back in Chesterton. I suspect that they'll need your help soon."

Again, Tomas felt like his weight was on his back foot. What did Ghosthands intend?

He was even more confused when Ghosthands turned to leave.

"Aren't you going to capture me?" he asked.

"I will. But your time is not yet." The quiet confidence in Ghosthands' voice sent a shiver down Tomas' spine.

"Then why come out here?"

"To give you the message that your friends are in danger. It is, as you know, the mission of the church to protect the innocent." He paused, then said, "Besides, after reading so much about you, I wanted to meet you in person. I had hoped that perhaps after all this time, I'd finally found an opponent worthy of my skills."

"Then fight me!"

Ghosthands shook his head, and Tomas was surprised to find the man actually looked sad. "There's no point. You're a weak man, Tomas." He turned his back on Tomas.

Tomas let the power from Elzeth fill his limbs. He leaped forward, eager to separate Ghosthands' head from the rest of his body.

F ifteen paces became ten, then five. Ghosthands gave no sign he'd even heard Tomas approach. Tomas' sword cleared its sheath, and he was too close for Ghosthands to do anything except die.

Then Ghosthands' back became his front, and there was a sword in his hand. Impossibly, it was closer to Tomas' neck than his own sword was to Ghosthands'. Tomas twisted, his defense broken in a single move. He knew he was too late, though. All Ghosthands had to do was snap his wrists, and Tomas would be close to dead.

The cut never came. Tomas kept twisting and his feet tangled up in the tall grass. He passed Ghosthands and fell on his side. By the time he was back on his feet, Ghosthands' sword was already back in its sheath.

Tomas blinked, trying to make sense of what had just happened. He held up a hand to his neck, but there was no cut there. In fact, it looked as if Ghosthands had never moved at all. "I told you, Tomas. You're weak."

"Why didn't you strike?"

"Your time is not now. Were you listening to anything I said?"

"There's no point in listening to a corpse." Tomas advanced. His sword was drawn, and Ghosthands' rested in its sheath. This close, there could be only one outcome. Tomas' cut was perfect, his body in harmony with Elzeth's power.

He missed.

His sword cut through nothing but air, and he wasn't sure why. Ghosthands still stood exactly where he'd been before. This time, at least, Tomas had enough dignity to remain balanced.

He cut again, and again he missed. Tomas, growing wise to Ghosthands' speed, continued the advance, letting one cut bleed into another.

He sliced nothing but air and grass. He backed up several paces, sword steady before him.

It reminded him of another warrior, deep under a mountain, who had been similarly difficult to defeat. Eventually, though, Tomas had killed him. Just as he would kill Ghosthands. He wasn't alone. "Narkissa, together."

He attacked again, and again he did nothing except amuse Ghosthands. He drove the churchman toward Narkissa. She had a clean cut at his back, but the fact didn't bother Ghosthands in the least. The assassin retreated from Tomas, growing ever closer to Narkissa.

She shifted her stance, bringing her hand to her sword and preparing to draw.

A few more paces, and they would have Ghosthands in a position he couldn't escape.

The moment came, and Tomas let out a shout of triumph.

But Narkissa never drew her sword.

Instead, she shook her head and backed away, her mouth uttering some silent string of denials. Tomas' heart sank.

The only one who didn't look surprised was Ghosthands. His voice was patronizing, as though he was a parent explaining something simple to a child. "She's near the edge of madness, Tomas. If she uses what little strength remains to her, she might lose the last scraps of her sanity. All of this would be for nothing."

Was she so scared of her sagani she wouldn't even draw her sword? Tomas struggled to believe she'd fallen so far.

Even if that was true, watching her back away still felt like a betrayal of the trust he'd put in her.

A small reflection of his own betrayal so many years ago.

Seeing her so afraid, so broken, made Elzeth burn even brighter.

Tomas would find the way to surpass Ghosthands. He always did. He would deliver the cure to Narkissa and offer some small repayment for the suffering he had caused.

Tomas cut, then cut again. He advanced relentlessly, but Ghosthands gave up ground willingly, always one move ahead of Tomas. "Don't you see, Tomas? No matter how hard you fight, no matter how hard you struggle, it doesn't matter. The least you can do is go save your friends before they're forced to endure a lifetime of suffering for aiding you."

Tomas swung too hard and lost his balance. Ghosthands stuck out his foot and tripped him. Tomas was back on his feet in a moment, but Ghosthands made no move to kill him.

Getting beaten was bad enough. But stomaching such a casual dismissal awoke in Tomas a rage he hadn't felt since he was a much younger man, a man lost in the world after the war had been taken from him. A man who had thought he'd found a new purpose in working for Hux.

"Are you finished yet?" Ghosthands asked. "I tire of this."

Tomas cracked. He rushed forward again, his anger and Elzeth's rage building upon one another until he was certain they would burn the entire world to the ground.

One more time, Tomas cut nothing but air. This time, Ghosthands retaliated, driving a fist into Tomas' stomach. The breath left Tomas' lungs, looking for more welcoming environments. None came in to replace it. His gut felt as though a charging bull had hit him.

Tomas stumbled back, swinging his sword with one hand while he clutched as his stomach with the other.

Ghosthands still didn't press his advantage.

Finally, Tomas gulped sweet air. He found his balance and attacked again. Ghosthands was here, in front of him, with the cure in his pocket. All Tomas had to do was cut him down.

Except that was the one thing Tomas couldn't do. No matter how fast his sword cut, no matter what combinations he strung together, his opponent might as well have been a ghost. It wasn't just his hands. His entire body seemed ethereal, immune to Tomas' steel.

Still, Tomas tried again, because what else could he do? He took a deep, shuddering breath and attacked again.

He didn't see the blow that knocked him down. One moment, he was swinging at Ghosthands' head. The next he was on his back, staring up at the sky.

He groaned and rolled to his hands and knees. Ghosthands stood close by, studying him skeptically. "Are you really going to try getting up?"

Tomas swore and pushed himself up. This time, he barely saw Ghosthands' boot as it kicked him. The force of the blow lifted him off the ground, and then he collapsed in a heap. He tried to get to his feet again, but his body refused.

Not only that, the last kick had been like a bucket of water dumped on top of Elzeth's flame. The sagani sputtered out and fell silent. Tomas imagined him curled up in a ball, licking his wounds.

This time, when Ghosthands walked away, Tomas let him.

Strong as his determination might have been, even he could face reality when it slapped him repeatedly in the face.

He couldn't beat Ghosthands.

Once the assassin was gone, Narkissa walked over to him. The fear on her face was gone, and she had a look on her face he'd seen too many times in the past. A smug satisfaction that reminded him of Agis.

She'd never been much for sympathy, but he was still disappointed when all he got for his trouble was two words. Surely, he deserved a bit more.

She extended her hand to help him up.

"Told you."

25

The two of them retreated over the rise. They were probably safe enough where they'd confronted Ghosthands, but Tomas had a powerful urge to tuck his tail between his legs and run away. He could well imagine the laughter the knights shared at watching their feared enemy defeated by one of their own. Ghosthands hadn't even had to draw his sword to finish the fight.

They took a seat on a small knoll where the sun could keep them warm. Tomas was in no mood to talk, and Narkissa obliged him.

The fight with Ghosthands was supposed to have answered the questions lingering in his thoughts. Instead, it had given him so many more.

One realization towered over all others.

He couldn't beat Ghosthands.

If the fight had been decided by speed, or some slight difference in technique, Tomas might have hoped for a different result the next time they crossed swords. He and Elzeth had stopped short of unity, a last bit of strength and intuition that might have bridged a narrower chasm.

But that wasn't the case today. He'd been bested as though he were a novice swordsman wandering into a sword school for the first time. Even unified, he would lose against Ghosthands.

He took a deep breath and let it out slowly. He'd lost plenty of battles in his life. Hells, he'd been on the wrong side of an entire war.

At least, that was what the government kept telling him.

But it had been a very long time since a single warrior defeated him with such ease. He'd gotten too used to being the strongest. Today was a valuable reminder that there was always someone stronger.

Fortunately, being weaker didn't equate to losing. It wasn't always the strongest sword that won. Sometimes, it was the smartest. Ghosthands had a weakness.

Tomas just had to find it, then exploit it.

As complete as his defeat had been, Ghosthands hadn't caused any serious damage. Tomas would carry bruises for the afternoon, but he counted himself lucky.

Every blow he'd taken was delivered with careful intent. Ghosthands wanted him to fight. He wanted Tomas to return to Chesterton, to experience whatever fresh torment he'd devised. A wiser man, or at least a more cold-hearted one, would have turned and walked away.

Narkissa and Agis were like stakes that pinned him in place, though.

"How are you?" he asked Elzeth.

"Napping," replied the surly sagani.

"What happened back there? I've never felt you get so angry at so little." It wasn't like Elzeth to get riled up by an enemy's taunts.

"Everything about that man sickens me," Elzeth said. "To be a host who hates a part of himself so much, and to be able to be so casually cruel..." He trailed off. "We've crossed paths with evil before, but that man is something else. He's a monster."

Tomas agreed, but didn't push any deeper. For now, he let the sagani rest. There would be a need for him soon enough, if Tomas guessed correctly.

He stood and brushed off his pants. The sudden movement startled Narkissa. "You're leaving?"

"Returning to Chesterton."

"That's what he wants you to do."

Tomas shrugged.

"You're more soft-hearted than I remember. Too much so. It's going to get you killed."

"Probably. But it's better than the alternative." He gave her a pointed glance.

His insult didn't bother her in the least. "We could leave it all behind. If I don't use it at all, who knows how long I might still have? Months, maybe. They could be wonderful months for both of us." He heard the promise in her voice, the blind hope.

The offer tempted him. They would be on the run from Ghosthands, but they'd be together. She wouldn't die alone, and he'd have more opportunities to atone for the sins of his past.

But Ghosthands knew him too well. He couldn't leave. Narkissa could, though. "Leave if you want. I won't go until I'm sure Agis is unharmed."

She swore. "You know, Hux used to worry about this."

"About the health of innkeepers?"

"About you developing a conscience. For a while, he thought that was what had happened, why you'd abandoned us. He couldn't believe it was simple cowardice."

The words stung, as intended.

Then he decided he didn't care. Narkissa's arrival had thrown his world into turmoil, but it had also forced him to confront memories he should have long ago.

Once, the past had held him tight. Regret and an unfocused desire to right the wrongs he'd committed had influenced most of his decisions. Slowly, as though he was prying one finger at a time from his heart, it lost its grip.

If Narkissa left, he'd be clear of it all. He forced the issue. "Are you coming with me or not?"

Narkissa didn't answer for several minutes. Then she shook her head. "No. I'm going to find a hole so deep not even Ghosthands can find me. And then I'm going to drink until my money runs out."

Her answer hurt, but the wound healed far faster than a shallow cut. He reached into his own pocket and pulled out the last of the coin he had. He tossed it to her. Then he took off Nester's pack and handed it to her. It still had a bit of food left in it. "Should help get you started."

For a long moment, they looked at one another, like two children competing to see who could go the longest without blinking. Tomas wondered if she was testing him, testing his resolve to see this to the end.

She broke first. "Would you come with me, please?" she asked.

He saw her in a different light then. She'd weighed her possible futures and decided she would rather run and cause what last chaos she could, while she could.

He supposed he shouldn't be surprised. Where others fought for glory, for riches, or for recognition, she'd always fought because it was fun. She didn't care for the world, and was determined to suck every bit of marrow from the bones of life as she could.

Some part of him had hoped her imminent death would change something, but he'd been a fool.

Tomas considered her offer one last time.

It didn't tempt him at all. It felt as though his chest were expanding, as though tight belts were being loosened, one after the other. He'd loved Narkissa once, in the madness of his youth. He still cared for her, and his heart broke at the future she faced.

"I'd fight for you, but I won't run," he said. "Never again."

She took his refusal better than he expected. "I had to try."

He held out his hand to her. "It's been good to see you, Narkissa."

And he meant it.

She took his hand, and he helped her to her feet. He looked at her for a minute, committing the details of her features to his memory. He searched for some words that seemed suitable for bidding her farewell, but none came to mind. Both of them had always preferred acting to speaking.

Tomas stepped forward and embraced her. Once again, he seemed to catch her by surprise, but she returned it quickly enough.

Finally, he tore himself away, bowed deeply, and turned toward Chesterton, leaving his past firmly behind.

26

Tomas walked through the tall grass of the prairie alone, with nothing but the dying wind and his thoughts to keep him company. Elzeth slept, and from the feel, wasn't planning on waking soon. He ran his hand along the grass, feeling the tips of the stalks brush and scratch against his palm.

He kept turning his head and checking behind him, halfway expecting Narkissa to be there, running to catch up to him. But every time he looked, he was still alone.

Why would she come? Tomas had never walked toward a more obvious trap, and unless he came up with some way of forcing Ghosthands to react to him, he had little chance of emerging alive and unharmed. If she had to choose between a short life and a slightly longer one, well, he couldn't entirely fault her for running. It seemed he was the one the church wanted most, anyway. There was a very good chance that if she kept her trouble to a minimum, they wouldn't pursue her.

He walked slowly, in no hurry to reach Chesterton. The

trap would still be there, ready to spring, whenever he arrived. He used the time to think and to plan.

Not that it did him much good. By the time the town once again came into view, he still hadn't come up with anything beyond "Don't die."

It was a good enough start, though. He settled into a comfortable patch of grass that he could observe part of the town from. The sun was down, but Tolkin hadn't yet risen.

Once again, the town seemed more like a freshly restored and painted ghost town than a place where real, living humans worked and slept. All the houses were dark, but Tomas noted light coming from the mission.

"Time to wake up, old friend," he said.

Elzeth stirred to life, like old embers under a gentle puff of air. "Would have been happy waiting for another day."

"Not sure Ghosthands will be quite so patient," Tomas said.

Elzeth's awakening sharpened Tomas' sight and hearing, and he looked over what little of Chesterton he could see. Nothing struck him as being unduly alarming, but he supposed it wouldn't be much of a trap if he could spot it from well beyond the outskirts of the town. Even with Elzeth's help, he couldn't see any movement in the streets.

Then he did. A cart, which looked so heavy that its axles were in danger of snapping, was inching out of town, pulled by two horses. Tomas saw the familiar figure driving the cart and could guess well enough what had happened. When it didn't look like anyone pursued the cart, he broke from cover and walked toward the road.

He waved when Leala saw him. She slowed the horses to a stop. "If you've got a lick of sense, you'll turn around and run the other way as fast as you can," she said.

"What happened?"

"Things started getting really spicy this afternoon. I had more visitors to my shop today than I've had in months, but they weren't looking to buy. They were looking for you. One young gentleman even brought me an awfully familiar rope and asked me if I'd sold it to you. When I said that I had sold it to a man and a woman traveling through here yesterday, he kindly informed me he'd be keeping it, to hang you with."

Tomas shrugged. "It is a sturdy rope."

Her eyes narrowed. "I don't think you understand. Near as I can tell, the whole town is after you, and I'm guessing it isn't for an invitation for tea. What did you do to piss them off so bad?"

"Sure you want to know? More you hear, the more danger you might be in."

She scoffed. "I already consider it fortunate I lived through the day. Thankfully, Edana was reasonable enough to convince the mob that I couldn't have known what you'd do when I sold you the gear. But I saw some looks that made me think it might be in my best interest to pick up my stubborn feet and make a living somewhere far, far away from here. So the least you can do is tell me what caused all the trouble."

"We broke into the mission and killed six knights."

Leala's eyes went as wide as the full moon. She swore under her breath. "Turns out, maybe I didn't want to know." Before Tomas could ask his next question, she hit him with hers. "Where's the other half of your party?"

Tomas decided he really liked Leala. Not too many people would accept the death of knights so casually. He was glad to see she was leaving while she still could. "When we couldn't find what we were looking for, we made a trip up to the fort. That was enough to convince her the thing we were searching for wasn't worth the trouble."

"And you think it is?"

"Not at all. But when we were there, we learned Agis might be in danger for hosting us. So I came back to tell him to get out of town."

"That's good of you, but I don't think he will."

"Still have to try. I don't think Edana is going to protect him for much longer."

Leala looked at him for a long time, some decision being balanced in the back of her mind. "I'll wait not far away, at least for the night. If you find him and can convince him to leave, he can travel with me."

Tomas bowed. "Anything I should know before I try to find him?"

"The town isn't as quiet as it looks. Everyone is up, gathered in the mission. Couldn't tell you why, but couldn't say I liked the feeling of it much. Feels like trouble."

"I think you're right. It's good that you got out when you did. Stay safe."

"I'd tell you the same, but I doubt that's in the cards for you."

"Rarely is," Tomas said.

Leala snapped her reins and urged the horses into motion. They started slowly, but eventually, the cart rolled forward again.

There wasn't much point in waiting and hiding. If the church had people on watch in the tower, they would have seen him talking with Leala. So, he stuck his hands in his pockets and moseyed down the road.

He paused for a moment once he was in town. No one leaped from the shadows to grab him. Nothing moved. Even the wind had stopped.

He ducked off the primary thoroughfare as quickly as he could, preferring the alleys between buildings. It made him easier to trap, but it kept him out of sight from prying eyes. Eventually, he found himself in front of Agis' inn. Candles and a fire lit the dining room, so Tomas assumed the innkeeper was present. He stepped in, stopping briefly to wash his hands. He didn't dare take off his boots, but he at least kicked the dust off them.

Agis' footsteps heralded his arrival, but when he came around the corner, he didn't seem terribly surprised to see Tomas in his inn. "Wondered if you might show up. Where's Narkissa?"

"We crossed paths with the man who's in charge of what's been happening here. It was enough to convince her she wanted no part of it."

"I imagine you've come to convince me to leave?"

Tomas nodded.

"My mind hasn't changed."

"I don't think your daughter's authority is going to protect you as much as you hope it will."

Agis gave him a smile filled with sorrow. "You don't have any children, do you, Tomas? No family?"

Tomas shook his head.

"She's worth staying for. I have to stay here for her."

"Even if it means dying?"

"Even then."

Motion in the streets caught Tomas' attention. Dozens of torches, coming from the direction of the mission, marched toward the inn. Tomas couldn't make out individual faces yet, but there had to be nearly a hundred people packing the street. "They're coming, Agis, and I can't stop them."

"I would never ask you to. Thank you for coming, but you should go now, before it's too late."

Tomas poked his head out the door and looked both ways.

Another crowd was gathered at the other end of the street.

It looked like "too late" had already come and gone.

Tomas' heart pounded as the mob approached. His palms sweated as he imagined the futures in store for Agis. Not to mention, if he didn't get out of here soon, his own futures looked even more unpleasant. He'd heard the occasional rumor of a church-led mob burning an unfortunate host at the stake, but he'd never believed them.

Watching the torches as they bobbed up and down in the street, the tales no longer seemed so farfetched.

But he couldn't leave without giving Agis at least one more chance to escape. The old man had done nothing wrong, and didn't deserve any of what was coming his way.

"Agis, I know you're all about making things right with your daughter, but you aren't going to make anything right with that mob at her back."

Agis remained unmoved, the torches now close enough Tomas could see them reflected in the innkeeper's stare.

He tried again. "That's not some rational group of citizens you can speak to. They're more like an untamed horse, ready to throw anyone and anything that tries to control them to the ground. If you confront Edana now, it's going to be dangerous for her, too. Come with me. You can always return."

Agis shook his head. "No running. Not for me. Not when my daughter is here. But you need to leave. I appreciate you coming back. It speaks to the quality of your character, but this, this is where our paths separate. I wish you the best on yours." He held out his hand, and Tomas took it.

"To you as well. Don't die on me."

Agis said nothing, and Tomas offered the man one last bow. Then he sprinted toward the back. There was another door, through the kitchen, that led to a small alley behind the building. Before long, the crowd would surround the exit, but one advantage to a mob was that they tended not to move too fast. Tomas closed the door silently and ran through the alley, away from the approaching danger. Then he turned to leave the town.

Elzeth said, "You sure you can live with that decision?"

The question brought Tomas skidding to a stop. Already, the regret of leaving was gnawing at his stomach. Agis had made his choice. He'd given Tomas every excuse. There was nothing to feel guilty about.

His guilt, unfortunately, had no interest in listening to any of the voices of reason shouting at it.

Agis' trouble was Tomas' fault. The innkeeper had sheltered them and fed them, even after guessing the mischief he and Narkissa had started. If Agis wanted to risk his life for his daughter, that was his own business. But he only had to risk his life because of Tomas.

"I thought you were supposed to be the reasonable one," Tomas said.

"I'm tired of running," Elzeth said. "If we keep

surrendering these minor battles, then soon there's not going to be anything left to fight for."

"Someday, we're going to have to sit down and have a real long conversation about you developing a conscience," Tomas complained.

"I blame you."

Tomas looked around. Despite his complaints, he was grateful he and Elzeth felt the same. Now he needed to figure out how to fight this war and stay alive.

It made little sense to come back the way they'd run. They'd only find an angry mob ready to hang him from a short rope. He also held out a small hope that the mob wouldn't attack Agis.

After all, Agis was still one of Chesterton's residents. They might not be as eager to turn on one of their own, and if Tomas was fortunate, he could make it through the night without bloodshed.

He looked up. If he could find a quiet vantage point, he could watch the proceedings and decide on the best course of action.

He didn't want to be on this side of the street. Far better to be on the other side, so that he was behind everyone as they stared at the inn.

Tomas ran, putting more distance between him and the mob. Once he was a couple hundred yards away, he turned back toward the street the inn was on. He stopped by the corner of a building, crouched low, and stuck his head out.

The mob had stopped outside the inn, surrounding it. As Tomas had expected, all eyes were on the building. He called on Elzeth and sprinted across the street.

A sigh of relief escaped his lips when he reached the other side. Given the lack of shouting, he figured the mob hadn't noticed his quick crossing.

He ran back toward the inn. A conveniently stacked set of crates behind another building allowed him to ascend to the roofs. Less than a minute later, he'd found a place where he could crouch in the shadows and watch the scene below.

More than a hundred townspeople had gathered in the street. Leala hadn't been exaggerating when she claimed the whole town had been in the mission. Tomas' eyes roamed over the assembly.

Most seemed like nothing more than average citizens. He saw several swords, a handful of spears, and quite a few bows. No rifles, fortunately. That was the one weapon, more than any other, that worried him.

The looks on their faces frightened him, too. He listened to men snarl threats and saw women brandish kitchen knives as weapons. The slim hope for peace he'd held onto faded.

His eyes settled on a clump of five people near the center of the assembly. Each carried more than their fair share of scars, and Tomas noted the way the rest of the mob gave them just a little more space.

A unit of knights, dressed up to blend with the rest of the town. Had Tomas been on the ground level, he didn't think he would have noticed. His stomach knotted tighter. Ghosthands wanted him here, and had prepared for him.

Perhaps returning had been more foolish than he thought.

He forgot, sometimes, how church culture revered the knights. To him, they were simply powerful warriors, dangerous even to one of his strength. To a staunch believer, they were the warriors who defended the faith, who fought to protect their way of life.

And he'd killed six of them.

Edana called out, her voice ringing like a church bell. "Come out, Agis. I won't ask you again."

Tomas saw movement inside the entryway, and Agis opened the door. He stepped into the chilly night, and Tomas thought he stood a head above everyone in the mob.

"Where is he?" Edana demanded.

"He's not here, daughter."

Tomas couldn't see Edana's face from his vantage point, but he saw the way her body tensed when Agis reminded her of the blood they shared. "We know he came back to town, and we know the only reason he'd come is for you. You befriended him, Agis, even after you knew what he'd done."

Agis stood his ground, and Tomas couldn't help but think of some of his memories from the war. How many lone warriors had he watched stand their ground as the enemy charged?

Agis' bravery matched any of those martyrs. If anything, it was even greater, because he'd had so many chances to leave.

When Agis spoke again, his voice was so soft even Tomas had trouble hearing him. "I'm sorry if I've disappointed you again, daughter."

Edana shook her head, then shouted to the crowd, "Search his place!"

Agis made no move to stop the townspeople as they poured into his inn. Maybe twenty entered, and from the cacophony that sounded from the open door, they weren't bothering to leave the place in better shape than they found it.

Their anger needed an outlet, and Agis' inn was the first casualty. The mob broke his windows and threw furniture out of them.

As if Tomas was hiding underneath a nightstand.

He clenched his fist as he watched Agis' daughter tear his life to shreds. The sight almost caused him to stand and shout, to draw the town's attention to him. But there was still some chance the night might not turn violent, that the townspeople would burn their rage out by destroying the inn instead of killing Agis. It was still too steep a price, but one Tomas would pay.

Agis' brave facade cracked as the destruction of his inn continued. He flinched whenever another window shattered, when another piece of furniture splintered. A tear ran down his face.

Even Edana seemed surprised by the vitriol of the mob she led. She took a step back and gently shook her head. Her body language told Tomas she hadn't understood what she had helped to start.

He couldn't find much sympathy in his heart, though. She was young, and foolish, but even she should have known.

The destruction dragged on. It seemed like it lasted half the night, but Tomas guessed it hadn't been more than ten minutes when the townspeople trickled out of the inn. Some carried nice pans and lanterns as though they were prizes. One by one, they reported they hadn't been able to find Tomas.

The crowd quieted. Expressions softened.

Tomas breathed easier. It seemed like the destruction of the inn had sated the town's desire for vengeance.

The decision fell into Edana's lap. The mob looked at her. In one direction, chaos. In the other, a chance for peace and perhaps even a slow healing. Tomas, like all the others below, was on edge as he waited for Edana to speak.

He crouched lower as Edana turned to address the mob.

"He's not here. Let us return to the mission and pray for the souls of our protectors, sent too early to the gates."

Tomas breathed a slow sigh of relief. It had been a terrible night, but even Edana saw reason. Agis would live, and Tomas could fade away and escape whatever plans Ghosthands had for him.

A lone voice shouted from the crowd. One of the knights. "You'll let our brothers and sisters die without seeking justice?"

A second voice joined the first, from another knight. "He protected a murderer! He's as guilty as the killer!"

It was a small shove, but it was all the crowd needed. The mob grew enraged again, and soon everyone shouted for Agis' death. Edana's eyes went wide, and finally, Tomas felt pity for the young woman. She'd had no idea, and just now saw what bitter fruit her faith had sprouted.

She didn't capitulate, though. She'd inherited some of the steel that made up Agis' spine. "Wait! He's an innkeeper! He shouldn't have to die for the crimes his guests commit!"

The knight who'd first pushed the crowd, who Tomas suspected was the knight commander, shouted back, "Whose side are you on? The side of the faith, or your sinful father?"

Edana found herself trapped. The crowd quieted as they awaited her answer. Her eyes darted left and right, and her last mistake was trying to find neutral ground. "He doesn't have to die!"

In a more reasonable town, her flock would have heeded her pleas for moderation. Here, though, all she received for her efforts were calls of, "Traitor!"

The shouts of the mob drowned her last pleas out, and soon she found herself betrayed by her own flock. Ropes appeared, and it looked like the mob was busy making two nooses.

"Well, so much for a peaceful resolution," Elzeth said.

Tomas grunted. Only one option remained, and it was the one he'd been hoping to avoid. "You ready for this?"

"Not even a little."

"Good." Elzeth burned brightly, and Tomas stood up, sucking air into his lungs. Then he shouted as loud as he could.

"You want justice? THEN COME AND GET ME!"

28

Tomas' sudden appearance froze the crowd in place, and dozens of faces stared at him with slack jaws. The hands knotting nooses stopped their deadly tying. Every voice died as they noticed the intruder.

The peace didn't last long. The knights were the first to react. They drew their swords and stabbed toward him, as though he would fall from the roof from fear alone. "Kill him!"

Tomas turned and ran. He sprinted up the sloped roof and down the other side as one lonely spear arced toward where he'd stood. Tomas leaped from one roof to the next as bodies packed the alleys beneath him.

His eyes darted forward, seeking a means to escape. If he avoided dropping to the streets too early, he should be able to outdistance his pursuit.

If not, he would have to fight his way out, which he preferred not to do. Horrifying as the town's behavior was, Tomas wasn't like the churchgoers. He didn't believe mistakes merited death. All he needed to do was distract the town's attention long enough that Agis could escape.

He wished he'd studied the town more closely. There had to be stables around somewhere. He wouldn't say no to a horse.

Fast as he was, he couldn't outrun a mounted rider over distance.

The townspeople discovered the stack of crates that had given him such easy access to the rooftops of their town. A handful of them scrambled to the roofs. They shouted at him, and Tomas waved in return. A few tried to coordinate with the townspeople in the alleys below.

Tomas waited. Once a small group had assembled on the first roof, they came after him, leaping from that roof to the one where he'd watched the mob tear through Agis' inn. Then Tomas turned and ran, jumping over another gap between buildings. He had two more roofs he could jump to before he'd either have to fight or drop. He hoped that gave Agis enough time.

The mob showed an impressive amount of organization. Several of the people who'd climbed to the roofs carried bows, and Tomas watched as they took aim.

Thanks to Elzeth, he had just enough time to drop flat when the archers released. Arrows split the air where his chest had been just a moment before, and Tomas reminded himself he wasn't dealing with young army recruits. Most likely, the archers were hunters, some perhaps with experience in the war. They weren't in the habit of missing.

Tomas scrambled on all fours. Maybe a dozen people armed with swords and spears chased him, jumping from one roof to the next. Tomas counted four archers on the first roof.

The numbers didn't add up. There were only a couple of dozen in the alleys below.

Did they think they had enough people to capture him?

Tomas glanced down as he leaped to his penultimate rooftop. A handful of townspeople stood in the alley. Not as many as he expected, though. They knew where he was. Why didn't they surround the building?

Tomas rolled as two of the archers released at the same time. Again, the arrows passed directly overhead. Another arrow brushed past his shoulder as he stood.

Tomas swore. He hadn't expected such a coordinated assault. This was a mob, after all. Shouldn't the roofs be filled with vengeful citizens clamoring for his blood?

The group with swords and spears advanced, leaping over a gap in ones and twos, preparing their assault as he ran out of space.

Tomas gave up his current building after less than a minute, leaping to the last roof. From here, he either had to fight through the group following him or drop to the ground. He looked down. There was a scattering of people below, most of them thrusting pointy things up at him, but the number didn't seem nearly high enough.

Tomas ducked down and scrambled on all fours as the archers released again. There couldn't be more than forty or fifty people after him.

The pursuing group crossed another gap, leaving them on the roof next to Tomas. They spread out as they advanced toward the final gap.

Tomas swore as an arrow brushed past his shoulder. He hadn't even seen it coming, too distracted by the thoughts piling up in his mind.

The group on the roof across from him made to jump. Which was exactly the moment that Elzeth added one more problem to Tomas' already extensive list.

"Where are the knights?" he asked.

Tomas swore. None of the five he'd identified were in the

group advancing on him, and none would be caught dead with a bow in their hands. Perhaps they were down below, waiting for him, but that made little sense. For all their character flaws, knights didn't let others wade into battle before them.

If they weren't chasing him, they had a different aim in mind.

The group pursuing him jumped across, crowding his current roof.

The quickest way back to the inn was across the rooftops, so Tomas launched himself toward the group as they charged.

Before the sides could meet, Tomas heard the crack underneath his feet.

Then he felt the structure give way.

Whoever had built this roof apparently hadn't built it for more than a dozen people sprinting across it.

Stuck in the middle of the collapsing structure, there was nothing Tomas could do to escape. A hole opened beneath his feet, and both he and his assailants crashed down.

Tomas closed his eyes, tumbling and rolling as the world shook. He tried to breathe and received a nose full of dust for his trouble. All he heard were shouts of surprise and the ear-splitting cracks of timber. Something punched him in the stomach, sending him careening in a new direction.

A wall, apparently sturdier than the roof, was kind enough to stop his descent.

When he cracked open his eyes, he was on his back, his feet sticking straight up, resting against the wall. Dust filled the air, but Tomas could just barely make out Tolkin's pale red light in the sky above.

They'd only fallen one level, and although he had at

least a dozen minor cuts and bruises, he seemed otherwise unharmed. He coughed as dust coated the inside of his throat, then rolled over and pushed himself to his feet. He'd come close to tumbling through a window.

Tomas glanced out the window at the street below, where his ground-based pursuers gawked at the disaster.

"Tomas!" Elzeth shouted.

He turned, just in time to see what had alarmed Elzeth. Tomas wasted a precious moment trying to understand why someone was flying at him.

Then it was too late.

The man tackled Tomas, his shoulder to Tomas' chest, muscular arms pinning Tomas' to his side.

That was the moment Tomas decided standing in front of the window had been a poor choice.

They went through the glass. Once again, Tomas fell. Elzeth channeled strength through Tomas' body, strengthening him for the impact to come.

When they hit, Tomas swore a mountain had snuck up on him and sat on his chest. For the second time that day, the air was knocked from his lungs, and from the feel, his lungs had packed their bags and gone searching for a more suitable home. The man who'd tackled him went tumbling away from Tomas, and Tomas didn't think he'd be getting up again soon.

Unfortunately, Tomas didn't have the luxury of taking a nap. The observers on the street took whatever pointy weapons they had in their hands and came after him.

He scrambled to his feet, thanking whatever fates watched over him that none of the knights had pursued him this far. He easily sidestepped the clumsy strikes, even as blackness crowded the edge of his vision.

Tomas slid through the first gap that appeared. Finally,

his abused lungs decided they were ready to work again, and he sucked in a breath of clean air.

The observers gave chase, and Tomas ducked as a digging fork, thrown like a spear, arced above his head. He turned into the first alley that led toward Agis' inn.

And found another group of pursuers rushing to meet him from the other end.

29

Tomas swore as he skidded to a stop. He glanced back and saw the pursuers from the street sealing the alley behind him.

The alley was plenty wide for one person, but not quite wide enough for two to walk shoulder to shoulder. He couldn't run around them, and they deterred him from running through them with an impressively wide assortment of pointy weapons leveled in his direction. He counted at least two rusty digging forks, one chipped sword, a homemade spear, two shovels, and one oversized kitchen knife.

"I don't want to hurt you." Tomas said. "Put down your weapons!"

His plea for peace fell on deaf ears.

Before long, he wouldn't have a choice, though. He'd rather not hurt them, but he had no plans to die here.

The group in front was smaller than the group behind, so he charged them. That, at least, stopped their advance. But their leader, a sturdy woman with one of the rusty digging forks, set her feet and prepared to meet him.

As she stabbed at him, Tomas leaped, planted his foot against one wall of the alley, and tried to jump over the group.

In his head, he'd imagined clearing everyone in one leap.

But he misjudged his angles, and his foot slipped off the wall as he propelled himself higher. He cleared the first woman, and the look on her face as he passed overhead was almost worth the whole trip to Chesterton. Unfortunately, that was the last part of his maneuver that went to plan.

Instead of clearing the men behind her, Tomas ran straight into them, his shins knocking into their shoulders. The four of them went down in a heap, but this time, Tomas had the advantage of landing on top of them. He half-rolled, half-tumbled over the cursing men and found himself on his feet behind the group.

The woman who had been leading them turned and thrust her digging fork at Tomas. He shuffled back, then turned and ran as the woman screamed for blood.

Tomas exited the alley and found himself on a small street that was empty, at least for the moment. He spent a precious second getting his bearings. Agis' inn should only be a few buildings away. Despite his recent unpleasant experiences, the alleys between the buildings were still the most direct route.

Angry citizens emerged from the alley behind him, and Tomas took off again. A homemade spear skipped off the packed dirt near his feet, and he had to jump so as not to trip over it. He sprinted for the next alley, the shouts of his pursuers letting everyone in town know where he was and where he was going.

Which, he reflected as yet another group appeared in

the alley ahead of him, meant he should have tried a less direct route to the inn.

He tried to climb up the walls, so that he could escape across the roofs, but a hand reached up and grabbed his foot. Tomas kicked, but then another pair of hands grabbed his other ankle. He pulled with all his sagani-enhanced strength, but not even he could lift so many people.

Besides, in a few moments, he'd have to dodge spears and knives in addition to hands. He let himself drop and found himself in the middle of a mob.

His position gave him one very important advantage. Everyone around him was trying hard not to stab their friends and neighbors. Tomas could strike anyone. He swung his fists and elbows wildly, connecting with plenty of surprised faces. After a minute, he cleared a space, presenting him with another choice.

If he drew his sword, he could cut his way through the crowd in just a few moments.

But for all the suffering they'd caused him, he couldn't quite bring himself to blame them. He still didn't want their blood on his hands.

So he attacked them empty-handed, sliding between attacks and delivering one blow after another. With Elzeth aiding him, it wasn't much of a fight. There were a few citizens who seemed like they'd gotten their basic training in the army, but with Tomas so close to unity, no amount of training would save them. As he passed, he was like a boat in the water, leaving a wake of defeated enemies behind him.

And then he was through the next group.

"Tomas!" Elzeth warned.

This time, Tomas didn't hesitate. He shifted sideways, and an arrow came straight down and buried itself near his foot. He glanced up and saw that two of the archers from earlier were standing near the edge of the roof. Now that he was clear of their friends, they had unobstructed shots. The first was nocking another arrow, and the second was taking aim.

Thanks to Elzeth, Tomas saw the exact moment the second man's hand released the string. Tomas slid out of the way, and the arrow missed by an inch.

Then Tomas was running again, hoping to break the line of sight before the first archer could fire again. He turned the corner of the alley just as an arrow ricocheted off the wall next to him.

Free once again, Tomas sprinted toward Agis' inn. For all the people he'd come across, it still wasn't enough, and he feared that every moment he wasted returning to the inn would be a disastrous one for the innkeeper.

Tomas emerged on the street two buildings down from the inn. In his immediate vicinity, the mob was gone. But they weren't hard to find. Tomas glanced down the street and saw the missing people. They had found a tall tree, which was already decorated with two taut ropes.

His gaze took in the entire scene in a second. There were the rest of the archers from before, in position on the rooftop. Their arrows were nocked and waiting for him to approach.

At a cry from one archer, the whole mob turned and spread out, like a sea dividing. It gave Tomas a clear view to the tree, where the five knights had gathered around the ropes. Agis and Edana were both there, nooses tight around their necks. They each stood on a short chair.

Edana's eyes were wide, her face pale even in Tolkin's red light. Her mouth moved, forming a silent prayer. Agis held himself stiffly, but there were tears running down his eyes as he stared at his daughter. When he saw Tomas, he gave the smallest bow of his head, as much as the noose would allow.

Tomas' stomach tied itself into a knot nearly as tight as the nooses.

One knight, when he saw Tomas, smiled and waved.

Then he kicked the chairs out from under the father and daughter.

30

___

There was no thought involved, not even a moment of internal debate. It never occurred to him he could just turn the other way. He wasn't even sure who initiated the union. It could have been him or Elzeth, because they both howled in agony as Agis and Edana fell.

The thin barrier separating host and sagani dropped, burned to ash in the purifying fire of their anger.

As soon as unity seized him, a familiar peace blanketed his mind. Unity allowed no space for thought. Tomas became an arrow launched from a bow. His urge to rescue Agis and Edana was a primal reaction, like a parent protecting their offspring.

Any noble thought of sparing the townspeople vanished.

Tomas sprinted forward, his feet light over the packed dirt of the street. The archers released their arrows, but he stepped to the side and the bolts buried their points into the dirt.

The mob closed ranks as he attacked.

He had time for one last look at Agis and Edana before the bodies of the townspeople broke his line of sight.

The knights had been deliberate in their hanging. Instead of a longer fall, designed to snap the neck and kill instantly, they'd only let the rope drop father and daughter an inch or two. Their death would come from the much longer and more painful method of suffocation.

They wanted him to attack. They wanted him to come to them, to make a mistake in his anger.

He didn't care.

The mob dropped a line of spears as the first rank of their defense.

Tomas drew his sword, slapping the spears aside contemptuously. None of his foes had training. They'd been given the weapons and had stuck the pointy end out as far as their reach allowed. Only one had the sense to draw their spear closer to their body, but by then it didn't matter.

Tomas was among them, and the whisper of his sword was the last sound his enemies heard.

None stood a chance. They were slow, and their numbers did nothing but give them a false sense of confidence. They were as likely to stab one another as they were to draw his blood.

They parted before his flashing blade, and he ripped a seam straight down the middle of the mob.

Amid the carnage, Tomas finally found the peace he'd sought for so long. In unity, there was no thought, no debate, no hesitation. His body, trained since childhood to wield a sword, became a mindless weapon. There was only move and counter, instinct and reaction.

He didn't know how many fell before the mood in the mob changed. He could feel their emotions, as though they were palpable things he could hold and shape. Before, their anger had almost matched his own. But as he fell among them, killing friends and neighbors, that hatred turned quickly to uncertainty.

It didn't take long for that uncertainty to turn to fear.

They realized, far too late, that their numbers meant nothing. The individuals who had been pushing to get to the front of the crowd turned tail and ran, shouting for others to do the same.

In what seemed like no time at all, it was just Tomas against the knights. They stood in a line between him, the innkeeper, and the priest. They attacked together, their blades red in the moonlight.

For the first time since his sword cleared its sheath, Tomas encountered resistance. His sword was turned aside as the masters in front of him parried his blows.

Tomas growled.

They were in his way.

One knight focused too much on Tomas' sword, and never saw the boot that shattered his right knee. The knight dropped in silent agony.

In different circumstances, Tomas would have taken a moment to finish the knight off. His defense had dropped, which was a rare moment to take advantage of. But the kicking forms of Edana and Agis filled his vision.

He leaped over the falling knight, breaking free of the circle of warriors that wanted to kill him. Two steps brought him to the hanging family. One cut from his sword brought them down.

Their hands had been bound behind them, and they both collapsed to the ground, unable to balance. Tomas needed to cut the ropes from their necks, but the knights were on him before he could. Three of them tried to drive him back while the fourth went to kill Agis and Edana.

Tomas refused to give up ground. He stood among the whirling storm of steel, suffering cuts but giving at least as good as he got. In less than a heartbeat, he was pushing the knights back. The fourth knight, seeing her comrades in trouble, decided she couldn't waste the time it would take to kill Agis and Edana.

It didn't matter.

Tomas let their strikes cut at him, sacrificing his body for quicker kills. He couldn't feel their cuts, but they died at his.

With every knight that fell, the battle became easier. By the time the knight who stood over Agis and Edana reached the fight, there was only one other knight left.

He didn't think he'd ever killed two knights so fast. He cut them down and turned his attention to the poor innkeeper and his daughter.

The first knight he'd hurt, the one whose knee he'd broken, wasn't content with being maimed. He threw a knife at Tomas from the ground.

Tomas watched it spin slowly through the air and caught it. He threw it back at the knight, leaving it embedded in the man's left eye.

Something punched him in the left shoulder. He looked at the arrow, wondering how it had gotten there. Then he pulled it out dismissively and raised his sword. He pointed it at the one archer who hadn't run when he should have.

The archer took one look at Tomas' bloody sword and decided that caution was the better part of valor.

He took off running.

Finally, the street was empty.

Tomas ran over to Agis and Edana and sliced the ropes from their necks. Both choked and coughed as air reached their lungs again.

Tomas took one last look around. The streets were quiet.

Not even the dying groaned as their lifeblood pooled in the dirt. They were well and truly alone. The need for unity had passed.

And yet, he didn't want to let go. Despite all his injuries and exhaustion, he felt a warm glow suffuse his body, as though he was standing right next to a fire on a snowy night. His mind was at rest. Overhead, the stars twinkled, pinpricks of light bright against his enhanced vision.

He felt the other half of himself struggling. Of the sagani trying to separate itself.

But letting go felt so wrong.

It was the sight of all the bodies that drove the first cold stake through the warmth that surrounded him. The recent past was nothing but a distant memory, but there were so many dead. Thoughts returned to his mind, riding on the heels of regret.

He'd never wanted to kill so many.

Hells, he'd never wanted to kill any of them.

It was just the separation Elzeth needed. The sagani took on the responsibility of building the wall between them, breaking unity.

Once cracked, the feeling of peace faded quickly, leaving, in its absence, an emptiness Tomas didn't know how to fill. He longed for unity in a way he never had before. But Elzeth, stubbornly, kept rebuilding the wall between them.

Tomas briefly considered tearing it down again, but couldn't find the desire. He'd spent his whole life as a host avoiding unity. But that wasn't what held him back.

Elzeth did. Tomas felt the sagani's worry and noticed the haste Elzeth used building back the barriers between them.

He couldn't ignore Elzeth's wishes. Not after all they'd been through.

So even though there was nothing he wanted to do less, he helped the creature rebuild the mental barriers that kept them apart.

The relief he felt from Elzeth almost convinced him it was worth it.

31

The battle over, at least for the moment, Tomas turned his full attention to Agis and Edana. Agis had pushed himself up into a sitting position, but Edana still lay where she'd fallen. They both breathed without too much difficulty, and except for the bruising already forming around their throats, were uninjured.

Although both of them needed time to rest and recuperate, they didn't have the luxury. Tomas had broken the back of the mob, but he couldn't guess how long it would be before it reformed. If he was fortunate, he'd scared them all the way back to their homes, deep under the covers of their beds.

But he wasn't willing to stick around and find out whether his hope reflected reality.

"You two fit to walk?" he asked.

Agis nodded, but Edana continued lying there, motionless except for the gentle rise and fall of her chest.

"We need to leave before anyone thinks about coming back," Tomas said.

Deep in his stomach, he felt Elzeth stirring restlessly.

Normally after a fight, the sagani preferred to take a nap until Tomas needed him again. Something bothered him, though. Unfortunately, Tomas didn't have time for the discussion.

Elzeth knew as much, too, which was the only reason he wasn't vocally complaining. But the sagani unsettled Tomas, distracting his attention and reducing his patience.

Edana remained still on the dirt, the cut fragments of noose lying around her prone figure. Her eyes were still as wide as when the noose had been around her neck, but Tomas couldn't guess what she saw.

Agis scooted over to his daughter and lifted her head so that it was in his lap. He held her close, but it was as if he was holding a stiff mannequin.

Tomas looked up and down the street. It was still quiet. He didn't catch any motion, not even in the windows or on top of the roofs. But the silence didn't ease his concerns. They didn't have time for this. "Agis, we need to go."

"I know, it's just—" He gestured at Edana.

"I'll carry her, if it comes to that."

That caught her attention. She bolted upright, and her wide eyes narrowed, and blazed with hatred. "You will not dare lay a finger on me!"

Right. Tomas guessed a "thank you" wasn't coming anytime soon, then. It didn't change what needed to happen, though. "Then you'd best be on your feet by the count of three. I didn't risk my life to save you just so you could throw it away."

Tomas supposed he could have been more diplomatic, but he liked Edana about as much as he liked ingrown toenails. He guessed he had the warmer feelings of the two of them.

The fire in her eyes burned even brighter. "And if I don't?"

"I'll knock you out and throw you over my shoulder anyway."

"Come, Edana," Agis said. "We need to leave."

"But they're my flock!" she said. "He killed them!"

This time, it was Tomas' turn for his eyes to go wide and his jaw slack. After all that, her mind was still on their side? He knew belief was as stubborn a human trait as existed, but "her flock" had hung her from a tree to suffocate. "If you want to head back to the mission, be my guest," Tomas said.

Agis shot him a glare, then turned back to his daughter. "They might have been your flock once, but they aren't any longer. They'll kill you if they see you again."

Tomas almost started the countdown, but the street was still quiet, so he let Edana have a few seconds to decide. The silence stretched out, one heartbeat after the next. Just as he was about to intervene, she nodded. Tomas breathed out a sigh of relief.

Slowly, the two got to their feet and let Tomas lead them out of town. He waited for some comment from Edana as they walked through the path of bodies Tomas had cleared, but none came.

Tomas was grateful. He'd never considered himself a man of peace, but even he was torn up by the sight of what he'd done. He averted his eyes, grateful for an excuse to stare at the rooftops and dark alleys between the buildings. Soon they were clear of the scene and making good time.

He made for the outskirts, taking the shortest path possible, eyes and ears alert to any movement that might indicate an effort to flank them. Fortunately, it looked as though Tomas had scared the town away. Before long they were out on the prairie.

Tomas walked a dozen paces ahead of them, constantly glancing back to ensure a mob wasn't forming on their tail. Chesterton was as quiet as ever, and if not for the flickering of candles in the windows, it would have been easy to believe the whole town was asleep.

Edana clutched her father's arm as though it were an anchor.

Seeing the headstrong woman leaning against her father sparked a small bit of sympathy in his heart. She'd believed with her whole heart, and she was just now understanding the dark consequences of her unquestioning faith.

Tomas hadn't been all that different after the war. He'd believed so deeply in the cause, he wasn't sure how to live in a world where his side had lost.

A bitter part of Tomas, who'd seen far too much of the shadowy underbelly of the church, wanted to rub her nose in it.

It wasn't his small amount of pity that stayed his tongue, though. It was the knowledge that nothing he could say would hurt her as much as what she'd already witnessed this night. With luck, tonight would lead her to repair her relationship with her father.

They found Leala's cart without a problem, and Tomas helped the pair into it. The axles groaned under the additional weight, but Leala didn't seem troubled by it. Once they were safe, Tomas went around to the driver's seat. "Thanks for this."

Leala patted the rifle near her seat. Tomas hadn't seen it before, but it looked well used. "Have no fear. If anyone does come after us, I'll keep us safe."

"Good. I'm not sure there's going to be any pursuit, though. I think they're going to be licking their wounds for a while."

She glanced down at his bloody clothes. "Looks that way."

"Town's population has gotten smaller since you left."

She snorted. "Sure you don't want to come with us?"

"No. I tend to attract trouble. Best if I walk alone for a while, I think."

"You probably speak true, there." Leala considered for a moment, then turned and rummaged in her cart. She pulled open a crate and grabbed something, then offered it to him. "A little something for the road, then."

Tomas' eyes went wide for the second time that night. "Is this—?"

"Sure is," she said with a grin. "They were supposed to be for someone prospecting way out west, but they got cold feet. They're all bought and paid for, though, and I figured someone like you might find a creative use for them."

"Indeed." He bowed deeply to her. "I think I can."

Leala reached back into her cart again, and this time pulled out something Tomas was even more interested in. It was at least two or three meals' worth of food.

With that, Tomas said his last farewells. Agis thanked him profusely, Leala waved, and Tomas liked to believe that Edana glared at him a little less fiercely than usual.

He watched them travel until they were a speck in the distance. Then he left the road, seeking a place where he could rest and heal from his final visit to Chesterton.

32

Tomas found a small depression, far away from the road, and collapsed into it. He stared at the stars, but they no longer seemed as friendly as they had earlier. The only thing heavier than his limbs were his eyelids, but before he closed them, there was a question he needed to ask. "We good?"

Elzeth still hadn't settled, not since the fight in the street. He hadn't spoken, either. Now, finally, Tomas felt a wave of reassurance. "We're good for now. Get some rest."

Tomas barely needed the encouragement. He found a comfortable position, closed his eyes, and fell asleep.

He didn't sleep long. When he cracked open his eyes, the sun was just rising over the horizon, banishing the last of the darkness.

He stretched, grateful to discover that while he slept, Elzeth had healed most of his injuries. The bruises and cuts had faded, and he felt more refreshed than he had any right to feel. "Thanks."

"You're welcome."

Tomas sat up. His stomach rumbled, reminding him it

had been nearly a day since he'd eaten. He grabbed the food Leala had given him. He smiled as he thought of the fiery shopkeeper and hoped that wherever she settled next, it would bring her more prosperity.

He ate slowly, savoring every morsel. Leala's food for the road couldn't compare to Agis' cooking, but it was a sight better than anything he would have hunted down today.

"What do you want to talk about first?" he asked Elzeth.

"I think it's all the same."

"How so?"

"The answer to one will influence the answer to the other."

Thanks to the food, Tomas was in a patient mood, so he waited for Elzeth to explain.

"Unity was different for you, too, right?" Elzeth asked.

Tomas grunted as he chewed on some dried venison.

"Same here. It's been a long time since I've desired anything so powerfully." Elzeth paused, slowly coming to his point. "It scared me."

"Why?"

"I…" Elzeth's voice trailed off. His hesitation made Tomas sit up a little straighter. After so long together, it was rare for either of them to hesitate about much of anything. "The longer we're together, the more the thought of unity scares me."

"Is it my breath?"

Elzeth swore at him. "I'm trying to be serious here."

"Sorry."

When Elzeth was sure Tomas didn't have any more sarcastic comments, he continued. "I like our arrangement. I enjoy being able to think, to plan, and to talk with you. When we unify, it feels like turning back into what I once was. Most days, I'm not very interested in that. But when we unified back in Chesterton, I craved that thoughtless oblivion."

Tomas shivered as he considered how Elzeth's experience mirrored his own. "We've always been able to break apart before," Tomas reasoned. "We will in the future, too."

"Will we? Not to doubt you, but I felt what it was like back there, and I'm not convinced you would have let go willingly, which only makes it harder for me. We feed off of one another's emotions."

"I hear you, friend."

Elzeth was firm. "I don't think you do. I think we should consider never unifying again."

That froze Tomas in place. "Never?"

"I know you're thinking about visiting the fort with the supplies Leala gave you. We're both thinking about the church cure and what it might mean. And I don't think for a second we'd escape that hells-cursed hole in the ground without unity. Ghosthands handily destroyed us last time."

"You don't think we should do it?"

Elzeth sighed. "I don't know. If Ghosthands and the church have something that kills sagani, I want to know. But I don't see our day ending well if we return."

Tomas sat in the depression, finishing the last of the food. He watched the clouds pass through the sky and let his mind wander. The crossroads before him loomed large.

Thoughts of the peaceful places he'd visited dominated his thoughts. Nester and his family, living a life close to the one he'd always imagined. And Angela's house. Places he would return to in a heartbeat if he could keep the people who lived there safe.

"If you were the one who had to choose, now, what would you choose?" he asked Elzeth.

The sagani was silent for a long time, but Tomas didn't press. They had all the time in the world to make this decision. Finally, Elzeth answered. "I would return to the fort." He sounded disappointed in his own answer.

"It's worth it?"

"It is."

Tomas nodded. "I agree. I don't know how we finish this war that we started, but until we do, we'll never have peace. Ghosthands, and the church that stands behind him, will pursue us until the day we breathe our last. We can't run from this."

"What about unity?" Elzeth asked.

"All I can do is promise that I'll try to remember to help split us again."

Elzeth didn't respond, but Tomas felt him stirring deep within.

Eventually, the sagani spoke what was on his mind. "Do you think Ghosthands spoke true?"

"About what?"

"Mastering his sagani."

Tomas shrugged. "I don't have the slightest idea what that means."

"Maybe he's found another way to be a host. A way that gives him more strength and speed."

Tomas didn't dismiss the idea out of hand, but it still didn't sit right with him. "I don't think so. Don't you think we would have stumbled upon it by now?"

"Not necessarily. We've spent so long with me resting and you trying not to use me, we didn't spend that much time exploring what we were capable of."

"Is it something you want to risk?"

Elzeth's laugh was bitter. "No."

"For what it's worth, I don't think he's better than us

because of how he hosts his sagani. I think he started out as a true sword master, then became a host. I suspect he was a knight before. Maybe one of their best. I'm good, but I was never a master."

It didn't feel like Elzeth was convinced, but without asking Ghosthands directly, there wasn't much they could do about it.

Tomas changed the subject. "How should we do it?"

"Wait until tonight, then introduce ourselves?"

Tomas lay back in the grass. With the sun warming the ground again, another nap was creeping up on him. He could use the rest if the night was going to be as exciting as they expected.

"Wake me if there's danger?" he asked.

Elzeth's answer was the same as it always was.

"Of course."

33

Tomas woke to the setting sun, fully refreshed. He stood, stretched, and worked the last vestiges of soreness from his body. "Nobody came to visit?" he asked.

"A few crows flew overhead and seemed curious if you were alive or not, but otherwise, no."

"Any signs of a search?"

"None that I noticed."

Tomas grunted. That didn't sit right with him. After the night before, he would have expected at least a bit of a posse. The lack of one made him feel as though he was still walking right into Ghosthands' traps.

Of course, Tomas planned on visiting the fort. It didn't take a strategic genius to predict that as being one of Tomas' most likely moves.

But was Ghosthands so certain in Tomas' actions that he wouldn't even try to find him? So little of the past few days made sense to Tomas. He'd killed enough knights to set the church back months, if not years. Why wasn't the whole might of the church in the area searching behind every tree and under every bush?

He arched his back and felt the vertebrae in his back crack. He sighed in contentment, then made ready to leave. "I really wish I knew what was going on," he said.

"That makes two of us," Elzeth agreed. "But I'm going to get some rest while you head toward the fort. A nap sounds good."

The sagani fell asleep instantly, which Tomas took as a good sign. The trouble between them wasn't resolved yet, but they were on the right path.

Tomas strolled slowly, but also walked straight toward the fort. He saw little point in hiding anymore. Any knights he encountered on the way were knights he didn't have to fight once he was inside the walls. But he didn't want to appear until the sun was down and night had fallen. He planned to attack before Tolkin rose. His sharper vision would give him that much more of an edge over the knights.

And he wanted every advantage he could get. Even without Ghosthands, there were enough knights in that fort that approaching it was nearly suicidal.

He timed his arrival well. The slight bowl around the fort came into view right about the time darkness fell over the land. Then he stopped. In all his preparations, he hadn't planned for this. Narkissa was relaxing in the grass, the rim of the bowl keeping her out of sight of the fort. She waved, and he picked up his feet and made his way toward her.

He stopped about ten paces away. They stared at each other for several long moments, as though it was a competition where the first one to speak was the loser. Tomas sighed. He didn't have time for her little games. "Why are you here?"

By now she should have been miles and miles away. Had

she really been here the whole time while he'd fought in Chesterton?

She said nothing. All she did was hold out her hand. It tremored, then twitched, violently. "I left, Tomas. Walked away, just like I said I would. Barely made it a mile before my whole body gave out on me."

"So you just came here and waited for me to show up again?"

She shook her head. "Actually, that part was a surprise. I thought you were gone for good after you abandoned me. I've been sitting here, watching the fort, trying to figure out a way in."

"You thought you could steal the cure alone?"

"It's what I do best."

Tomas couldn't argue with that. "You come up with anything?"

She shook her head, bitter. "There isn't a single crack to exploit. I've been watching for a night and a day, and those knights are just about the most disciplined soldiers I've ever come across. I haven't seen so much as a gap I could slide through. They constantly watch the walls. None of the guards suffer from a lapse in concentration, and when they're not on the walls, they're training constantly. I don't think a fly could sneak through there without being cut down."

Tomas listened to her with a grin growing on his face. If Narkissa hadn't been able to think of a way to sneak into the fort, there wouldn't be one.

Fortunately, he brought gifts.

He showed her what Leala had given him. She stopped her tirade the moment she laid eyes on what he'd brought.

"Well," she said. "I guess that changes things, doesn't it?"

"Care to try them out?" he asked.

"You always know how to bring a girl the nicest things." He held one out to her, and she took it. "Would you believe I've never actually used one of these?"

"Really? There wasn't as much of it around back then, but I figured for sure you would have tried it since."

She shook her head. "No. Hux floated the idea a few times, but it was always too noisy for our tastes. We weren't usually trying to attract so much attention."

Just then, her hand trembled again, and she lost her grip. Tomas' gift tumbled to the ground. Narkissa nearly leaped back when it hit. Tomas picked it up.

"On second thought," she said, "perhaps now isn't the time for me to be playing with new toys. I'm afraid I'm going to have to let you have all the fun for now."

He reached out and grabbed her hand. "We'll figure something out."

The words felt hollow, even to him.

A look passed over her face, too quickly for him to decipher. Uncertainty, perhaps? Given how far she'd deteriorated in just over a day, he supposed it made sense. "Are you sure you want to go? I wasn't planning on meeting you here, and I'd do it alone. If I find the cure, I'd bring it back."

She shook her head. "No. Even like this, I can help. I have to. I just need something to snack on before we leave. Would you mind grabbing the pack?"

Tomas didn't. He grabbed it and set it between them. Then he glanced up at the rim of the bowl. "Aren't you worried about the knights?"

She laughed. "They know I'm here. I sat out in the open all day today. They don't care about me."

He heard the scorn in her voice. Maybe Ghosthands

knew, but he'd hurt Narkissa worse by ignoring her than he could have sending half his knights in pursuit.

They dug into the pack Tomas had left with Narkissa to help her flee. There was still a little food left, and they both nibbled at it. Then she pulled a flask out of the pack and took a sip, sighing in contentment. She offered it to him, and he took a sip, too. It tasted like whisky, but with a bitter aftertaste. He scrunched up his face. "What was that?"

"You don't like it?"

"I mean, I've had worse." Then he frowned. "Wait, where did you get that?"

The pack had come from Nester, and there'd never been a flask in there. The giant had been kind, but not so kind as to pack whisky.

She was rummaging around in the pack. Her movements seemed clumsy, even for her worsened condition. She pulled out another flask and took a sip before answering. "I'd had it hidden on me."

Of course she'd keep her liquor hidden from him, even after days of travel. He supposed he understood. Their trip to Chesterton hadn't exactly been made under the most auspicious of circumstances.

Then his frown deepened. There was something wrong, but his brain was suddenly very slow. He felt as though he needed another nap, even though he'd spent most of the past day and night resting. He shook his head to clear it.

The thought finally took shape. She couldn't have hidden it. After he'd captured her, he'd searched her thoroughly. He was about to point that out, but his tongue felt heavy in his mouth.

Too late, he understood. He realized the true reason she was out here, and the reason the knights hadn't cared that she sat outside their fort. He called for Elzeth, but it felt as though he was calling through an infinite void, a cave with no end.

He thought he heard the sagani, his voice nothing more than a whisper on the wind, too far away to help.

And then his world went black as he took that nap his body so desperately desired.

34

Tomas returned to awareness slowly, like he was an injured warrior crawling to the safety of consciousness. His first thoughts were sluggish and disjointed, a blending of dream and reality in which one was nearly indistinguishable from the other.

The cold steel around his wrists served as the anchor that pulled him back to the real world. He opened his eyes and was unsurprised to find himself in a jail cell. He blinked, trying to clear the sleep from his eyes. A small amount of sunlight trickled in from a tiny barred window set high in the wall. Night had passed, and it was at least morning.

He groaned as his head pounded. Whatever Narkissa had drugged him with, it wasn't without its after-effects.

He let out a quiet string of curses long enough to burn the ears of even the most veteran warrior. He aimed his most vehement curses at Narkissa, but he saved a few near the end for his own foolishness. Despite his promises to Elzeth, he had trusted her again. He'd dropped his guard, just a little, and that was all she needed.

He was a fool, and worse.

But that wasn't news. He'd known that for most of his life already, so he got past it and focused on the problem at hand.

"Elzeth?" he asked.

"Here."

"What happened?"

"You were dumb enough to drink something she gave you."

"In fairness, she drank from the flask first." His memories returned, one quick flash after another. He remembered her clumsily searching through the pack for her second flask. That must have been the antidote to whatever she'd given him. He snorted, then supposed he had to give her at least a bit of credit. She'd poisoned herself first so as not to give him any warning.

Clever. But she always had been.

"Where are we?" He suspected the answer, of course, but hoped Elzeth could confirm it.

"Within the fort. As near as I can tell, they had this cell underneath one of the corner towers."

Tomas cursed himself one more time. He'd escaped out of plenty of cells, but given that Ghosthands was probably in charge of this one, he wasn't liking his odds.

Elzeth let him stew in his regret for a while, then said, "Tomas, there's something you need to know."

"What?"

Before the sagani could answer, the hallway door outside his cell opened. A familiar silhouette appeared.

Ghosthands stepped to the other side of the bars. He radiated a sense of satisfaction. "Tomas, glad to see you're finally awake."

"Sorry to keep you waiting. That last drink was stronger than I expected."

The corner of Ghosthands' lips twitched, as though he was about to smile, but his facial muscles had forgotten how to perform the movement. "Defiant to the end. I like that. I suppose it serves you right, though. Alcohol is a curse nearly as dangerous to society as the demon you carry around inside of you."

"You mean that we carry around."

Ghosthands shook his head and looked as though he was about to launch into another monologue, but Tomas stopped him with a question.

"Where's Narkissa?" Tomas hadn't expected that to be his first question, but it escaped his lips before he could think about it.

"I'm surprised you care."

"Let's just say I have a list of people I need to visit, and she worked her way to the top last night."

"I'm certain. You'll be happy to know I gave her the vial I showed you earlier, and she scampered away like a squirrel with a particularly tasty acorn."

"Is it actually a cure? Does it kill the sagani?"

Ghosthands didn't answer for a moment. Tomas thought he saw a flicker of debate cross the man's expression, but it settled quickly. "Her sagani will die soon enough, but no, there is no cure. At least, not that we've yet found. I filled the vial with water."

Tomas closed his eyes, letting the weight of the confession settle on his shoulders. Suspecting the truth and having it confirmed were two very different feelings.

Narkissa hadn't faked the severity of her symptoms. The madness was taking her, slowly devouring its way through her body and mind. He supposed it gave her some justification for the betrayal. Not that he forgave her, but he understood.

She would be dead soon. No two ways about it.

Even after her betrayal, he found the inevitability of her death saddening. In part, she'd become a host because of him, and now it would cost her life.

It took him too long to realize that Ghosthands was staring at him, studying him as though he were an insect under some scientist's microscope.

"What?" he asked, his voice hoarse.

Ghosthands gave a small shrug. "You regret the loss of Narkissa's life, even after she betrayed you. Even though everything I've read about you talked about your irrational decisions, your... softness, I'm still surprised to see it in person. Somehow, you act more human than any other host I've ever come across. Remarkable, considering how long you've been a host."

"I'm just as human as you."

"But I'm not human."

Ghosthands issued the statement with such calm certainty, it felt like a gut punch. "Of course you're human."

"No." Ghosthands spoke slowly, as though explaining a simple concept to a particularly dense child. "I'm a monster. Not a monster like you, but a monster nonetheless. Perhaps the most important difference between us is that I know what I am."

"How can you say that?"

"How can you not?"

Tomas frowned.

"How many people have you killed over the years, Tomas? How many lives have you destroyed? Just this week, you came into Chesterton and have done your best to wipe it off the map. Are those the actions of a human being? Because I don't think so."

Tomas glared, but it didn't bother Ghosthands in the least.

He didn't like the direction of this conversation, so he changed its course. "What comes next?"

"You've done everything in town I could have asked for," Ghosthands said. "So our work here is done. The knights are finishing the construction of a reinforced wagon, a prison on wheels. Once it's complete, we'll parade you through Chesterton and then head back east. There are buildings full of church scientists who want to pull you apart and cut you open until they can figure out what makes you work. We might not have a cure yet, but soon, thanks to you, we might."

The only part of the answer that surprised Tomas was the first part. "What do you mean, 'all you could have asked for?' I killed your knights and believers."

"Exactly." Ghosthands didn't elaborate, drawing the moment out. "Haven't you figured it out yet?"

Tomas had no idea, but kept his mouth shut.

"Despite our growth, the church is attacked on all sides. The old ways still linger, despite our efforts to enlighten the masses. Our wealth attracts corruption of all sorts, and even the government fears our power and tries to topple us in ways that grow less subtle with every passing year."

"Could have fooled me. Church seems plenty powerful from where I sit."

"That's because your vision is so small. The Holy Father is worried that all these forces, nibbling on us both from within and without, will be our downfall. Peace is wonderful for our coffers, but we need more to keep the flame of faith burning brightly. And you've provided that. Back east, with fewer hosts and few wild sagani, people have forgotten how dangerous this world is. You, and everything you've done here, will remind them. Even now, we have the newspapers flooding into Chesterton. We've hired artists to paint the scenes of martyrdom. You'll do more to recruit new warriors and believers than anything I could have ever said or done."

Ghosthands pretended to applaud. "And the best part? It was all your choice. We don't even have to lie. All I had to do was spread one rumor here, threaten one heathen there, and the monster within you rose to the occasion."

Tomas' stomach twisted. "You wanted this?"

"I want a future where everyone believes the truth, Tomas. Where everyone has accepted the redemption the Holy Father offers. It is unfortunate so many new names had to join the list of church martyrs, but again, I know what I am. I'm the monster that will bring this world its ultimate salvation."

Then, to Tomas' horror, Ghosthands did smile. "And thanks to you, that day is now much sooner at hand."

35

Ghosthands left, but Tomas barely noticed. The weight of Narkissa's fate was nothing compared to the burden of the truths Ghosthands had just dropped on him. As sharp and deadly as the man's sword was, his words were no less dangerous.

He'd wondered, of course. Why sacrifice so many when there seemed so little need?

He never would have guessed that the sacrifice would be the point. That it had less to do with his personal battles, and more about a quiet war being waged across the nation.

Fool didn't even begin to describe him.

Elzeth had no patience for his regrets. "Whenever you're done wallowing in pity, we have things to talk about."

"Like what?"

"Like the fact that Narkissa's betrayal isn't entirely what you think it is."

Tomas swore. "We're in a prison cell, in Ghosthands' control. What should I be uncertain about?"

"She left a key to your manacles in your socks."

"What?"

"After she poisoned you, we talked." Elzeth paused. "Well, she talked. With you out, all I could do was listen. She apologized and explained."

"Any surprises?"

"No. She was desperate for the cure."

"Could have just asked."

"She knew you would have preferred to fight for it. She also believed Ghosthands would suspect a trap if she somehow captured you on her own. This was the only answer she came up with."

Tomas grumbled under his breath.

"She didn't trust Ghosthands, though, and she felt bad about what she believed she had to do. That was why she took off your left boot and sock, put a key between your toes, and then put the sock and boot back on. She hoped it would at least give you a chance."

Tomas took a deep breath and fought his frustration. It would do him no good. When the knights had taken him in, they'd stripped him down to tunic, underwear, and socks. But now that Elzeth mentioned it, Tomas wiggled his left toes and felt the key there, placed in the gap between his big toe and the next.

"Well, that gets us out of the manacles. We still have to find a way out of the cell."

"It gives us a chance," Elzeth said. "If any guard is foolish enough to come close to the bars with the keys, you can surprise them. They just threw your clothes and sword in the hallway's corner, so if we can get on the other side of the bars, you'll be armed in no time at all."

Tomas stretched out as far as the chain connecting his manacles to an anchor in the wall allowed. Elzeth was right. All his stuff was right there. Not that he could get to it, but it was there.

"What about Leala's gift?"

Elzeth snorted. "Narkissa took it, of course. Didn't think she'd leave that behind, did you?"

"No. I suppose not."

Tomas went to work, contorting his body so that he could pull his sock off, retrieve the key, and then pull the sock back on. He decided, for the moment, to leave the manacles attached. He didn't know how often the knights would come in to check on him.

Once he completed that task, though, he had nothing but time to think, and thinking brought him no joy. Few of his thoughts were pleasant. Finally, he couldn't keep them to himself any longer. "Do you think he's right?" he asked Elzeth.

"About what?"

"About what we are. Are we the monsters here?"

Elzeth's answer wasn't as immediate as Tomas would have liked. And the answer wasn't as reassuring, either. "Maybe."

The answer did nothing to improve Tomas' mood. "What would you have done? Would you have let them hang Agis just for the sin of letting us sleep under his roof for a night?"

"Of course not."

"Then what else would you have done?"

"I don't know."

Tomas slumped against the wall of his cell. His thumbs ran across the calluses on his palms and he closed his eyes.

He couldn't balance the weight of Agis' life against the churchgoing citizens of Chesterton. Any attempt at justifying or rationalizing the events of that night was nothing more than a hollow excuse.

No matter how the night had unfolded, it would have been a tragedy.

If there was any certainty to be found, it was that no part of that night needed to have happened. Ghosthands had orchestrated the events like a master conductor.

If he lived through the next few days, he could figure out how to carry on with the memories of Chesterton. They were still too fresh, too raw for him to deal with. For now, he latched on to the one fact he was certain about.

He was going to kill Ghosthands.

He only needed to figure out how.

Fortunately, the knights seemed content to give him plenty of time to plan ever more elaborate schemes. A knight would wander through every ten minutes or so, no doubt part of their regular guard duty. Tomas sat along the wall in his cell, hands hidden behind him. One particularly alert guard asked to see his manacles, and Tomas hid the key beneath his rear, twisted, and turned so the knight could see his hands remained locked behind him.

No matter how long he planned, though, he couldn't figure out any reasonable way to beat the assassin.

It was maybe an hour later when Elzeth interrupted his musing. "Does the nexus bother you at all?"

"No. You?"

"It's making it hard for me to rest."

Tomas felt bad he hadn't been paying more attention to the sagani. Now that Elzeth admitted to being unsettled, Tomas felt as much in his stomach. He'd been so distracted by thoughts of revenge he'd ignored Elzeth's problems.

The nexus was yet another complication, and one more concern he didn't have the space in his head to consider properly. He'd barely given it a thought since Elzeth had first mentioned it to him. But it was the other reason the fort was here. Perhaps the original reason.

This was the longest they had been around a nexus ever since their adventures with Franz and the others. Even that time they'd only had brief exposures. "What's it like?"

"It's hard to describe." Elzeth paused, considering. "I think it feels most like how you felt returning to Angela's place the last time, before we left Razin. Or returning to Nester's after working all day in the fields."

Tomas' heart ached at the references, but he understood. "It feels like coming home." He swallowed the lump in his throat. "Is that what you want?"

Elzeth didn't answer for a long moment. "I want to follow the call, and yet everything that I am fears what would happen if I did."

Tomas grunted. "But we already know, don't we?"

They did. When they had first touched the nexus, it had healed them from almost certain death. But it had also almost torn sagani away from host, killing them for good. "Should I be grateful there's some thick bars between us and it?"

Tomas felt the creature's amusement. "No. As we talked about, I'm not ready to leave."

"Good. I'm not ready to say goodbye."

The pair lapsed into a comfortable silence, the same silence they had enjoyed while walking hundreds of miles across the west.

The sun rose and fell, and apart from the frequent visits of the knights, little changed. He rested when he could, catching short stretches of sleep throughout the day. He listened to the sounds of the construction of the wagon that would eventually carry him away, and from what he could hear through the small window, it sounded as though they would leave at first light. If he was going to escape, he needed to do so soon.

He still didn't know how. The knights were cautious, and none of them wandered close enough to the bars to attack.

Then, as night fell, he heard the distant sounds of a horse galloping fast. The knights responded with all the efficiency Tomas would have expected. Heavy boots trampled on the wooden beams above Tomas' head as they ran to the wall.

He took advantage of the distraction, using the key to unlock the manacles from his wrists. He shook them out and rubbed them to bring the feeling back into his hands.

There was only one person who could be riding the horse, and he smiled as he thought of Narkissa galloping toward the fort, Leala's gift in hand. She'd be furious the cure was a lie.

Then he swore to himself.

She probably had Leala's gifts in her hands. And she was furious.

He walked over to the corner of the room farthest away from the exterior-facing walls and crouched down into the corner. "If you wouldn't mind?"

Elzeth grunted and flared. He strengthened Tomas' body.

It seemed silly, embracing such strength while hiding in a corner, but he hoped it would protect him from the fatal wounds that might otherwise follow.

Somewhere above, a voice shouted, "Bows!"

And that was the last thing Tomas heard before his world exploded.

36

Tomas covered his ears and curled into the tightest ball he could. He felt like an opossum curling up and playing dead. Hopefully Narkissa didn't make his act a reality.

Despite his precautions, when the explosion crashed over him, he felt as though he was at the epicenter of the blast, arms spread out in a welcoming embrace.

The cracks of thick timber served as percussion on top of the screeching of metal as the bars bent under the sudden, unexpected pressure of the tower collapsing. Splinters and debris pelted Tomas' back. The entire event crescendoed with a ground-shaking crash he felt through the soles of his feet.

As soon as the shrapnel stopped pummeling him, he stood up and turned around. His ears rang, but that was a small price to pay for being alive.

It had been a close thing, too.

As near as he could tell, Narkissa had thrown a bundle of Leala's dynamite right at the corner of the fort. The tower had fallen, bending the ceiling of Tomas' cell down. Had it bent much more, it would have crushed him.

Thankfully, the collapse of the tower ripped part of the cell door from its hinges. Tomas stumbled forward and squeezed through the gap.

He decided to celebrate his newfound freedom by putting on some pants. He ran to the end of the hall, threw on his clothes, and grabbed his sword. A moment after he finished, two knights flung open the door connecting the hallway outside the cell to the courtyard beyond.

They seemed more surprised to run into Tomas than he was of running into them. The surprise cost them their lives. Tomas' blade flashed out of its sheath, and they dropped to the ground like sacks of rice.

Then the world vibrated again underneath his feet.

He grinned. Narkissa hadn't used everything to blow up the tower. Still, he suspected Leala's gift wouldn't last much longer. For a moment, he regretted not having the opportunity to use some himself.

He poked his head out through the open door the knights had just come through and blinked at what he saw. The inside of the courtyard, which he assumed had been spotless just this evening, was now littered with debris and bodies.

In the center of the courtyard, there was a large wagon with thick walls. It was, he figured, the wagon that had been built to carry him back east.

It wouldn't be going anywhere soon. One axle had broken in two, and two of the wheels were split in half. The wagon rested almost on its side, and Tomas laughed out loud at the thought of Narkissa destroying a full day's worth of work with a single throw of dynamite.

His mirth vanished as another explosion rocked the

walls, tossing several knights into the air. From the way their bodies spun, limp, he guessed they were dead long before they hit the ground.

He didn't care about the knights dying. It was, in his opinion, what they should be best at. The manner of their deaths bothered him, though. He didn't like bows and hated rifles. They were unclean weapons, a way of fighting that lacked all honor.

Dynamite was even worse.

It didn't matter how strong of a sword you were when your enemy was throwing dynamite. There wasn't a cut or block in the world that would save you from its explosions. A lifetime of skill paled in comparison to the destructive power of dynamite. A child with one stick and a match was as dangerous as a whole unit of knights.

He pushed his doubts aside. Dishonorable as it was, Leala's gift had saved him from his cell. Now it was time to put that freedom to use.

The knights concentrated their defenses on the walls. Four knights on the west wall fought still, holding bows and trying to kill the lone rider on the other side. From their curses, Tomas suspected the effort wasn't going well. He didn't doubt the knights were passable archers, but it was dark and their enemy was throwing dynamite.

Like him, their true skill was with a sword in hand.

As another explosion erupted in a corner of the courtyard, Tomas wondered if he was seeing the end of the knights. The end of swords. What was the point in a lifetime of study when one could pick up a rifle and bypass the years of effort?

That, he decided, was very much a thought for another time.

Tomas searched for any sign of Ghosthands, but the

assassin wasn't anywhere to be found. Besides the knights on the wall, there were three knights in the courtyard, desperately trying to stamp out flaming debris near some barrels. He squinted, and it took him a moment to understand why they fought those particular flames with such enthusiasm.

He saw no one else.

The knights on the wall were his first priority. Their deaths would let Narkissa know he was alive. Then, if she wanted to run to safety, she could.

Tomas ran, taking the stairs to the top of the wall three at a time. He killed the first knight before the poor soul even knew his prisoner had escaped and now stood behind him. The second fell as he turned, and the last two found themselves woefully unprepared to fight a swordsman in their midst with only bows in their hands. As the last knight on the wall fell, Tomas heard a violent curse from below.

His first thought was that the language wasn't very becoming of knights. He looked down and saw the fire spreading below. It ate at the barrels, and the knights looked torn between running for their lives and redoubling their efforts.

The knights, never lacking for courage, chose to fight the fire with even more determination. Tomas grinned as he turned to the prairie.

He saw Narkissa riding a dark horse at breakneck speed.

He waved, then held out an outstretched hand. Hopefully, Narkissa would understand.

She did. She rode in close, then let go of the reins and used both hands to light something. Tomas saw sparks as the fuse lit, and she tossed it up to him as she rode underneath.

Tomas snatched it out of midair, amazed to see so little

of the fuse left. He twisted, turned, and threw, hoping he could deliver Leala's gift to its destination in time.

The knights were still fighting the flames when the stick of dynamite landed on top of the barrels. Tomas dropped. No matter how eager he was to watch, he didn't want to be exposed when the dynamite exploded.

A moment later, the explosion shook the fort once again. Tomas swore as he felt the walls creak and sway underneath, and he wondered if he had accidentally destroyed the entire fort.

Then the rumbling subsided, and when Tomas looked up, he couldn't help but laugh. He had blown a hole in the wall's side big enough that the armored cart could have driven through it.

There was no sign of the knights that had been near.

A glow to the side caught Tomas' attention. He looked over to where the knights had built a door and a small passage into the wall. His explosion had knocked the door and part of the passage open, and a very familiar blue glow came from inside.

Ghosthands and two more knights finally appeared from the last building standing. Despite all the chaos, their movements were calm and unhurried.

Tomas spoke to Elzeth. "You ready?"

"Not in the least."

Tomas smiled. "No point in anything less than unity, right?"

Elzeth hesitated, and for a brief moment, he worried Elzeth might fight him.

He needn't have worried. Elzeth burned brighter. "Just remember your promise, okay?"

Tomas nodded. "I'll do my best."

Then thought slipped away as unity took over.

The icy rage Thomas had felt before grew even stronger now. All he wanted was to kill the man standing in the courtyard below.

He leapt from the walls, landing softer than a feather amidst the chaos.

Then he strode forward, ready to kill a monster.

37

There was no discussion, no preamble. Ghosthands hated Tomas, and Tomas returned the feeling with interest. They advanced toward one another, and their swords danced impossibly fast on the moonless night. The first exchange opened a cut on Tomas' forearm. He felt the steel slice flesh, but no pain followed. They passed again, and again Thomas emerged with blood dripping from a new shallow cut.

Retreat was never a consideration. Wounds bleeding freely, Tomas advanced again. At times, his assault was so powerful he drove Ghosthands back.

But never for long.

Somehow, Ghosthands always found a way to turn the tide, to put Tomas once again on his back foot. Tomas hadn't drawn so much as a drop of blood.

Even in unity, he wasn't enough.

But his path had been set, and he would walk it until the end. Ghosthands would permit no retreat.

Ghosthands parried one cut and kicked Tomas hard in the stomach. He stumbled backward and coughed up blood.

He stood up straight, but Ghosthands didn't pursue. Exhaustion caused Tomas to sway, and thoughts trickled through the blazing fire of unity.

Ghosthands held his arms out wide. "You can't beat me, Tomas. No mere host can."

Tomas knew it was true. Perhaps, as he'd guessed earlier, Ghosthands was simply the better sword. Perhaps the church's assassin had found some way to squeeze even more strength from the relationship with his sagani. Tomas couldn't guess how, but the result was the same.

He couldn't find the space in his heart to care. He'd never expected to die as an old man in his bed. Dying at the feet of a powerful enemy was among the best ends he could ask for.

Tomas shook out his limbs and took a new stance, settling his pounding heart and his thoughts.

One last memory of Narkissa broke through the blazing fires of unity. They'd just robbed a stagecoach, and Hux and the others were off enjoying their spoils. A mood had come over Tomas, and he'd climbed to a roof to stare up at the stars.

Narkissa had broken away from the festivities below to join him. She'd kissed him deeply, her breath smelling like expensive whisky.

Tomas no longer remembered what he'd said. He recalled her face. She'd called him boring then, too.

But she lay down next to him. He let her use his arm as a headrest, and together they spent the night staring up at the stars.

Tonight, Tomas looked up to see the same stars, and was comforted.

She didn't have long to live, but he hoped she enjoyed the time remaining to her.

He let unity consume the memory, and he attacked Ghosthands one last time.

Just before they met, the sound of a galloping horse distracted the attention of all the remaining warriors in the courtyard. Tomas and Ghosthands turned in unison.

Narkissa rode through the hole in the wall Tomas' stick of dynamite had created. The horse leapt over flaming wreckage. The knights, who had been fanning out to surround Tomas, turned to face the new arrival.

Narkissa never slowed the horse. Something sparked in her hand, and Tomas, knowing Narkissa better than anyone else in the courtyard, turned to run. He was already sprinting away from Ghosthands and the two knights when Narkissa dropped the stick of dynamite at their feet.

There was little cover to choose from. The only thing near was the wagon which was supposed to serve as Tomas' prison on wheels. He scrambled up and over, jumping to the other side as the knights and Ghosthands fled in the opposite direction.

The dynamite exploded a heartbeat after Tomas landed on the other side of the wagon.

The wagon lurched, but protected Tomas from the worst of the explosion. The moment the explosion faded, Tomas broke from cover, searching for the assassin and the two remaining knights.

He found one knight easily enough. She hadn't reacted quickly enough, and the dynamite had killed her. The other was crawling toward the northwest corner of the fort. It looked like one of his legs was shattered, but he dragged the bloody limb with him.

Any hope that Ghosthands had suffered the same fate was quickly dashed when Tomas saw him striding toward Narkissa, who'd ridden the horse to the northwest corner of the fort. They'd gotten away from the blast, but the sound must have startled the horse, because Narkissa was struggling up from the ground. The horse stomped around Narkissa, but she rolled successfully away.

A glance told Tomas that Ghosthands hadn't escaped without wounds. He bled from several cuts and walked with the slightest of limps, favoring his right leg.

Tomas snarled and chased after Ghosthands.

Ghosthands heard him coming and turned.

Once again, the battle was joined. This time, it was closer. Tomas forced Ghosthands to give up space. The churchman backed up, growing closer to Narkissa with every pass.

Would she fight this time? Or would her fears control her?

Then Ghosthands stopped retreating.

Though it should have been impossible, he stood his ground, his blade inching closer and closer to Tomas. Tomas slid back one step, then another.

Ghosthands' blade defied every law of nature Tomas understood. It was always in front of him, seeking blood, no matter what he tried.

A high-pitched battle cry halted Ghosthands' advance. He stepped aside as Narkissa entered the fray, her sword passing inches away from Ghosthands' neck.

She'd come to help.

Tomas stepped forward, not wasting the opportunity Narkissa had given him.

Together, they created a wall of sharpened steel that no one should have been able to survive. They advanced steadily, but somehow Ghosthands stayed ahead of them. The battle was even, but not for long. Tomas felt himself slowing, felt his exhaustion and his wounds getting the better of him.

He dug deep, finding some small spark, and redoubled his efforts. They drove Ghosthands back and back some more. Narkissa even scored a shallow cut, sending a surge of hope briefly into Tomas' chest.

But it was all for nothing. They were two hosts at unity and they still couldn't beat him.

As Tomas slowed, the tide turned. Ghosthands stopped retreating and started pressing his advantage. Tomas didn't know how it was possible, but Ghosthands refused to die.

Tomas never saw the punch that shattered his nose and knocked him two steps out of the fight.

Narkissa, never a fool, jumped back to avoid Ghosthands' singular attention.

Ghosthands smiled again. "Thank you, both, for the challenge. I'll admit, tonight has been the most fun I've had in a very long time. But it must come to an end."

Tomas couldn't continue to hold on to unity. Elzeth still burned bright, but it wasn't the all-consuming fire Tomas needed to beat Ghosthands.

He shook his head. What was he thinking? Not even unity mattered.

All that was left was to die.

Then, in a corner of his vision, he saw a pale blue glow.

He risked a glance back. He could see the nexus, and it gave him an idea. A wild choice, but what else was left?

"Elzeth?" he asked. "The nexus?"

The sagani didn't answer at first. Belatedly, Tomas realized he might have just offered Elzeth an escape. The odds of Tomas living to see the morning were slim at best. If they touched the nexus and Elzeth left, at least one of them would continue on.

"Let's try it," Elzeth answered.

They didn't have time to discuss further. Hells, Tomas wasn't even sure they were fast enough to reach the nexus before Ghosthands cut them down.

Narkissa shifting her weight from one foot to the other caught his attention.

She could help, but it would very likely cost her everything.

He had no choice but to ask. "Narkissa! I need you to fight him for a moment. Then I can help."

Tomas wasn't sure if he was telling the truth, but he hoped he was.

She had every reason in the world to doubt him. More than anyone alive, she knew the cost of trusting him.

She barely hesitated. She stepped toward Ghosthands, placing herself between Tomas and the assassin.

Tomas turned and sprinted away, toward the nexus.

Narkissa watched him run away, just as he had so many years ago.

But she stood her ground. She threw everything she had at Ghosthands. She drove him back for a heartbeat, and then Ghosthands realized Tomas' destination. He cut Narkissa down in two passes. She fell to her knees, her sword dropping from her hands.

Her fight had bought him a ten-pace head start.

Tomas hoped it was enough.

38

Tomas sprinted into the shattered passageway. A few shallow stairs were cut into the ground, and Tomas took them three at a time. This close, the power of the nexus made the hairs on the back of his arm stand up. He reached out his hand and touched the uncut glowing stone.

The moment his fingertips made contact, the world around him faded. Power flowed through his body, stitching together his wounds and replenishing his strength. From past experience, he knew to let his body relax, to let the power flow through him.

Deep in his gut, Elzeth roared, fighting against the walls of Tomas' flesh like a caged animal. Tomas felt the nexus pull at Elzeth, welcoming him with open arms. Elzeth fought the pull, resulting in a twisting feeling in Tomas' stomach. The feeling worsened until Tomas thought he might vomit.

Then Elzeth relaxed and the pain faded.

The warmth of the nexus ran up Tomas' arm and enveloped him.

He couldn't feel Elzeth anymore, and at first, Tomas feared the sagani had finally left him.

He didn't care. Thanks to the nexus, he floated in an ocean of bliss. He was one part of something much larger than him. Something far more powerful, far more ancient, than he had ever imagined.

His conception of time faded. Lifetimes of serenity passed in less than the span of a heartbeat. Some awareness of the world remained. He knew, though he couldn't say how, that Ghosthands rushed to kill him.

But the fearsome assassin moved as though he ran through a tunnel filled with syrup. Tomas felt no rush, no hurry at all.

The space he found himself in was beyond language, and yet, Tomas was certain of everything he experienced.

A choice lay before him.

If he wanted, he could remain. He was welcomed. The peace he'd traveled so many miles to find was here, right in front of him. It had been his to seize whenever he wanted. Even now, memories danced through his thoughts, and he observed them one at a time. He watched that fateful night when he abandoned Narkissa in the bank, and for the first time in his life, it carried no regret.

He could remain connected to this source forever. Ghosthands would cut him down, and it wouldn't matter at all.

But he saw the truth. Knew what he would do even before he was conscious of the decision.

He wanted to fight.

Tomas couldn't say why, but something deep within him refused to accept peace. He and Elzeth had debated this before, but Tomas had never seen so clearly.

He would keep fighting to change the world. He would

fight for the Franzes, the Nesters, and the Angelas until his last breath.

He'd even do the same for the Narkissas in the world.

In this place, though, the decision carried no weight. He couldn't feel regret for any choice. Though he abandoned the one thing he claimed to want more than anything, he couldn't even summon a moment of doubt. Everything was as it was, and it was perfect.

Tomas pulled his hand away from the nexus.

His body hummed with strength. His sword crossed with Ghosthands', and for the first time, Tomas drove the assassin back alone.

He felt as though the world was paper-thin. As though the nexus had shown him something deeper, more real.

He felt as though he was fighting inside a dream.

Thought fled once again. Tomas didn't know if it was unity, or something else.

He couldn't say if he was faster, or if Ghosthands was slower, but Ghosthands' techniques no longer intimidated him. Tomas saw the way Ghosthands' weight shifted, and finally could predict how his enemy would strike.

Armed with that knowledge, Tomas couldn't help but defeat the assassin. Every pass drove the man back farther until he was retreating up the shallow steps into the courtyard.

Tomas pursued, but with every step, he moved farther from the dream and deeper into the reality he'd always known. Ghosthands moved faster with every swing of his sword, and soon, they were at parity. Tomas cut and fought with every ounce of strength he possessed, but his body no longer responded like it had moments before.

Then he was being driven back once again.

He snarled and raged. After everything, he couldn't lose!

But Ghosthands and his sword disagreed, and their argument was the most compelling one. No matter how Tomas raged, it wouldn't change the result.

With every pass, Ghosthands came closer to finally killing Tomas.

Then he caught a glimpse of motion out of the corner of his eye.

Like a wraith, she moved so silently he didn't even hear her.

Narkissa leaped into the battle. Injured as she was, she had no chance of hurting Ghosthands. But she caught them all by surprise when she threw herself bodily at the assassin.

Forced onto his back foot, Ghosthands stabbed out at her. The sword went through her stomach and out her back. But before he could pull the sword out, she wrapped her hands around his wrists, holding him with all the strength left in her body.

In unity, Tomas gave the sacrifice no thought. All he saw was his target, defenseless for a precious heartbeat. He stepped into the space Narkissa had made for him.

Ghosthands tried to defend by lifting Narkissa up with his blade and forcing her between him and Tomas, but it was too much weight, and Tomas was at unity. Tomas cut open Ghosthands' face, a cut intended for his neck that barely missed. Then he cut Ghosthands' arm, opening up a gash near the left shoulder.

Ghosthands snarled and pulled once more at his sword, this time with more force.

Narkissa let go, and the sword practically flew out of her. Ghosthands stumbled back, sword rising as it came out easier than he expected.

Tomas followed, cutting at Ghosthands' wide-open torso. Ghosthands stepped back, but not fast enough. Tomas cut across the man's stomach, a deep wound. Fatal, to anyone who wasn't a host.

The fight was over. No matter how good Ghosthands was, he couldn't fight through an injury like that. Not against Tomas, held tight in the bonds of unity.

Someone forgot to tell the surviving knight, though. During the battle he'd apparently managed to calm down Narkissa's horse and mounted it even with the broken leg. With one strong arm, he picked up Ghosthands as he rode toward the same hole that Narkissa had used as an entrance.

Tomas howled as they retreated. Then he took a step toward the wall, intending to chase after them.

He stopped.

His prey had escaped. His pack was still here. He looked down at Narkissa.

The sight of her was enough to break him out of unity. He started building the wall between him and Elzeth. Elzeth helped, and though he didn't speak, Tomas felt the sagani's relief.

He took a deep breath and looked at his hands. They remained steady. Then he knelt down next to Narkissa, amazed at what he saw.

The final stab wound from Ghosthands was bad enough. By itself, it would have almost certainly been fatal for anyone but a host. Narkissa might have survived it.

But Tomas had forgotten about the cuts she'd taken delaying Ghosthands in the courtyard. He'd cut her up good, opening enormous gashes along her chest, stomach, and legs. He didn't know how she had even moved to intercept Ghosthands at the end. It shouldn't have been possible.

She coughed, more blood than air. "How is it, doctor?"

"Fatal," he said. Hosts could heal a great number of

wounds, but despite what Ghosthands believed, they were still only human. Narkissa would die before her sagani had enough time to heal the fatal wounds.

She made a sound, which might have been a laugh, but it came out as another bloody cough. "But really, doc, tell it to me straight."

Tomas looked her over, mind racing to see if there was something he could do. What limited healing he knew was useless here. "Why did you come back?"

She coughed again. "Dying alone sounded less fun than killing Ghosthands."

"I'll never be able to repay you." He bowed down, pressing his forehead against the ground. "Thank you."

"I'll expect you to buy me a beer on the other side of the gates."

Tomas reached out and held her hand. It trembled, and Tomas was grateful she was still coherent.

Elzeth got Tomas' attention. "The nexus."

Tomas cursed. Already, he'd forgotten about it. It had healed him from wounds just as grievous. It could do the same for her.

Then he froze. There was one enormous problem. "Her sagani would have to stay."

"She's dying, Tomas. Either way, it saves the sagani inside of her, but there's a slight chance it might save her, too."

Tomas turned his focus back to Narkissa. "We might have a way to save you, but it's risky. If you touch the nexus, it might heal you."

"But?"

"But it will also try to pull your sagani out of you. Not sure what happens to the sagani, but if it leaves, you'll die. You'll have to hold onto it if you want to live."

She thought for a moment, then weakly nodded. "It's worth a shot."

Tomas squatted down and picked her up in his arms. Again, he thought about how light she'd become. He carried her, almost as if she was a child, down toward the nexus.

It didn't take him long to reach the glowing stone. He set her down beside it, not wanting to be in contact with her when she touched it. He had no idea if the connection traveled through bodies. "All you have to do is touch it," he said, "and then hold onto your sagani."

She nodded, but instead of touching the stone, she reached out and grabbed his hand. Tears were running down her face. "Thank you."

Tomas swallowed the lump in his throat and bowed his head.

"Don't leave me, okay?" Now, she sounded like nothing more than a frightened child.

"Never again."

That brought a smile to her face, and some of her usual attitude returned. "I think this new Tomas is growing on me. A bit of a bore sometimes, but I suppose that's a sign of old age."

He chuckled, the sound scratching at his throat. When he spoke, his voice was hoarse. "You should probably touch that nexus before you die making speeches."

She squeezed his hand, and the tears returned to her face. "I don't want to die."

Tomas squeezed her hand, then brought it to his lips and kissed it. "Believe it or not, I don't want you to, either."

For a moment, he thought she'd say something more, but she held her tongue.

She smiled at him, then let go of his hand.

She reached out and touched the nexus.

Her body arched, and she let out a bloody scream. Tomas watched, amazed, as the wounds on her body closed in front of his eyes.

It was working. He held his breath, watching the skin heal as though it had never been cut. Her breathing evened out, and she no longer sounded as though she was drowning in her own blood.

Then her body went slack, and the wounds stopped closing. Her hand, which before looked like it had been glued to the crystal, dropped.

Tomas stared for several long moments, not quite comprehending.

Then he bowed his head and wept.

39

The hole wasn't as deep as he would have liked, but it was deep enough to keep her body from predation. Not that she would have cared much, anyway. She'd always viewed funeral rites as something deeply silly. He had no trouble imagining her lecturing him on the pointlessness of it all.

She was already dead, after all. She couldn't be bothered to care about what happened with her body.

Tomas had never been able to convince her that the rituals were more for the living than for the dead.

He didn't know where he was, exactly. He'd taken a shovel and a horse from the fort. After wrapping Narkissa's body in some sheets from the barracks and securing it to a horse in the knights' stables, he'd left the fort and rode in a random direction. Eventually, he stopped the horse and started digging.

He stepped back and looked at the freshly turned dirt.

It had taken longer than he expected, and it wasn't until the sun was peeking over the horizon that he finally finished covering her up.

He'd buried her near a tree and wondered if that would be enough to serve as a marker for her tastes. Eventually, he unsheathed her sword and drove it into the ground. He figured she would have liked that.

"I feel like I should say something," he confessed.

"I think she knew how you felt," Elzeth said. "You can't ask for more."

"I could ask for her to still be here." He couldn't quite keep the bitterness from his voice.

"I'm sorry," Elzeth said.

"Don't be," Tomas said. "I know what you meant, and you're right." He looked down at his hands. They remained steady.

"I don't want to keep losing everything I care about."

Elzeth was silent for a moment. "But you will. It's what makes life precious."

Tomas heard the subtext loud and clear. "You think I should return to Angela?"

"Eventually, yes. I fear we won't be able to soon, though."

"Ghosthands will keep hunting us. Even though he succeeded in Chesterton, he didn't kill us."

Elzeth agreed.

Tomas looked down again at the grave. Narkissa had always appeared at the crossroads in his life. Once, after the war, as he searched for a new purpose. And now again. He bowed toward the grave and held the pose. "I'm sorry I couldn't save your life. But I promise, that if we do meet on the other side of the gates, the first beer is on me."

Before Chesterton, Tomas had been on the run.

But no longer.

Eventually, both Ghosthands and the Holy Father would realize they'd made a mistake in pushing Tomas as far as they had. His anger burned, a companion almost as constant as Elzeth.

A high-pitched screech came from above. Tomas looked up, surprised at the sound. A sagani, taking the shape of a bird, seemed as though it were wreathed in flame. Tomas' throat tightened. "Is that—" And suddenly he lost his voice.

"I don't think so," Elzeth said. "It can't be." But he didn't sound nearly as certain as his words made him out to be.

Tomas watched the bird circle several times above him. Then it dove, passing just a few feet above Tomas before pulling up and taking to the sky again.

It circled twice more before coming to a soft landing on the overturned dirt of Narkissa's grave. Then it cocked its head to the side and looked at him like it was an owl.

It screeched loudly, then took off again, dust billowing beneath its powerful wings. Tomas watched until it disappeared off in the distance, and he felt lighter.

It was free now.

Then he turned and looked down at the grave.

He hadn't been so certain about his own choices in a long time. But her return to his life had given him a clarity he'd long been lacking.

No longer would he run away like prey.

Moving forward, he would hunt the church down to the ends of the world.

THE ADVENTURES CONTINUE!

Top o' the morning!

I hope that wherever you are in the world, and whenever it is you're reading this, that you're doing well.

First, as an author, let me thank you for reading *Wraith's Revenge*. Whether this is the first book of mine you've read or my twentieth, I hope that you enjoyed it. There have never been more ways to be entertained, and it truly means the world to me that you choose to spend your time in these pages.

If you enjoyed the story, rest assured the Tomas' and Elzeth's next adventure isn't far off. Keep an eye out for the next book, releasing soon!

And if you're looking to spread the word, there's few better ways to support the story by leaving a review where you purchased the book!

Thanks again!

Ryan

STAY IN TOUCH

Thanks once again for reading *Wraith's Revenge*. I had a tremendous amount of fun writing this story, and am looking forward to writing more of Tomas and Elzeth.

If you enjoyed the story, I'd ask that you consider signing up to get emails from me. You can do so at:

www.waterstonemedia.net/newsletter

I typically email readers once or twice a month, and one of my greatest pleasures over the past five years has been getting to know the people reading my stories.

If I'm being honest, email is my favorite way of communicating with readers. Whether it's hearing from soldiers stationed overseas or grandmothers tending to their gardens, email has allowed me to make new friends all over the world.

Email subscribers also get all the goodies. From free books in all formats, to sample chapters and surprise short stories, if I'm giving something away, it's through email.

I hope you'll join us.

Ryan

ALSO BY RYAN KIRK

Saga of the Broken Gods

Band of Broken Gods

Last Sword in the West

Last Sword in the West

Eyes of the Hidden World

Oblivion's Gate

The Gate Beyond Oblivion

The Gates of Memory

The Gate to Redemption

Relentless

Relentless Souls

Heart of Defiance

Their Spirit Unbroken

The Nightblade Series

Nightblade

World's Edge

The Wind and the Void

Blades of the Fallen

Nightblade's Vengeance

Nightblade's Honor

Nightblade's End

Standalone Novels

Blades of Shadow

The Primal Series

Primal Dawn

Primal Darkness

Primal Destiny

ABOUT THE AUTHOR

Ryan Kirk is the bestselling author of the *Nightblade* series of books. When he isn't writing, you can probably find him playing disc golf or hiking through the woods.

www.waterstonemedia.net
contact@waterstonemedia.net

 facebook.com/waterstonemedia

 twitter.com/waterstonebooks

 instagram.com/waterstonebooks

Milton Keynes UK
Ingram Content Group UK Ltd.
UKHW041458180324
439705UK00002B/497